Bonnie MacDougall has been writing fiction for more than 40 years. She was also a professor of English for all those years, at several private schools or colleges in the New York area. Now retired, she is a Professor Emerita. She has a Ph.D. in English Renaissance literature from Columbia University, New York. She lives in Vero Beach, Florida, with her husband, Donald Durie Grein, Jr. where she has been active in civic projects that support racial equity and inclusion. She has several grandchildren, two cats, a dog, and a garden, always a garden.

To my sweet swain, my ever-faithful, Donald Durie Grein, Jr.

Bonnie MacDougall

SOMETHING TERRIBLE ABOUT LOVE

AUSTIN MACAULEY PUBLISHERS™

LONDON * CAMBRIDGE * NEW YORK * SHARJAH

Ordering Information
Quantity sales: Special discounts are available on quantity purchases by corporations, associations, and others. For details, contact the publisher at the address below.

Publisher's Cataloguing-in-Publication data
MacDougall, Bonnie
Something Terrible About Love

ISBN 9781638298786 (Paperback)
ISBN 9781638298793 (ePub e-book)

Library of Congress Control Number: 2022917380

www.austinmacauley.com/us

First Published 2022
Austin Macauley Publishers LLC
40 Wall Street, 33rd Floor, Suite 3302
New York, NY 10005
USA

mail-usa@austinmacauley.com
+1 (646) 5125767

A denizen of writing groups, I've found none to match the Tuesday Writers, part of the Laura (Riding) Jackson Foundation, in Vero Beach, Florida. Susan Lovelace, facilitator of the TW, finds the best in work presented; she also finds nuances no one else saw. She has been my generous reader. Jacque Jacobs, Ph.D., has been my reader and slices into the text with sharp-eyed points. Michelle Wheeler, member of my Close-Read group, will go to the ground for a point her writer's eye deems critical. As well, I thank Nina Dockery, Ed. D., Carla Giambrone, Ph.D., Karen Ambrum, LMFT, Jeanne Selander Miller, Stephen Chase, M.D., who affirmed the medical validity of my research. Thank you all. Others read and gave responses that changed or affirmed parts of the early drafts of my manuscript. Thank you, Judy Frisch Oldfield, Ann Colucci, Michael Redmond, Ph.D., and Brett Klein. I want to mention former students: Ranya Elfawwal, Qiana Mayne, Nia Morris, Diamond Grant Perry, Brendan Walsh, Muhamad Zaben. Each embodies unique nuances of life that enrich mine. Thank you. The furthest reach of my indebtedness and gratitude, to Pete Clements, sailor and novelist, author of The Latitude and The Last Floridian. I have learned from every word he has spoken or written, especially in his crackling critiques or lyrical approval of my writing. Thank you, Pete.

Table of Contents

Chapter One

"I'll have to deck him," Helen Baird, 54, said under her breath.

As twilight fell on Broadway in Manhattan, Helen jerked her body back and forth inside her leather jacket, trying to get free from the boyish-looking NYPD officer holding her. Facing her, he clenched her arms tightly against her body.

Helen yelled loudly, "Let go of me!"

"Hold still, lady!" The NYPD officer, no taller than 5'7" had trouble controlling 5'9" Helen.

Passers-by at the corner of 84th Street and Broadway stopped to watch the entangled twosome.

A slurred voice rose from a gathering group. "Look at that! Dancing with cops!"

"Move on," the NYPD officer shouted toward the voice, never taking his eyes off the woman he barely held captive.

"Tell me your name. Nice and calm and slow," the officer said.

Above the din of honking, tires screeching, hot voices arguing, and surrounded by the odor of pork fried rice from the take-out behind them, Helen screeched, "Let go of me!" She tried to stomp on the officer's foot but missed.

"Hey! Don't make things worse," the angry officer yelled.

Helen didn't answer. Her eyes were focused over the officer's shoulder as far down Broadway as she could see. Arms trapped against her body, she tried to knee the officer, but he jumped back in time to avoid her knee.

"None of that, lady!" the officer said to Helen. "I'm holding you for attempted assault on a police officer and on that young woman."

"Attempted take down! Points, bitch!" the same alcohol-drenched voice shouted from the crowd.

"I told you to move on," the officer shouted over his shoulder.

Helen raised her head. The officer saw one cheek dampen from steely eyes as she tried to glare at him.

"I'll try to help you, lady,"

She bucked sharply.

"Let me go!" Her voice was urgent.

"Look, whatever she took from you, lady, it's gone. She's gone," the police officer said.

Traffic at the corner stopped abruptly as the light turned red. A light blue Dodge Charger pushed into the center lane, scraping the side of a gray Toyota. A short graying man jumped out of his Toyota and barreled toward the Charger where a red-headed girl about eighteen sat cowering.

"What the hell you doing?"

Helen, still trapped by the officer on the sidewalk, went on her tiptoes to look again as far down Broadway as she could.

Couples coming from a nearby movie theater passed by, their voices in soft analysis of the re-enacted drama they'd just seen.

"Come on, princess. Kick to the head!" the goading slurred voice shouted at Helen.

"Name, lady?" the officer asked again.

A traffic cop's whistle, blown a few blocks downtown, hung in the air.

Helen glanced at the cop who held her, and looked away quickly.

She slumped slightly as she screwed her eyes to focus her long-distance vision.

The police officer restraining her adopted a sympathetic tone.

"How about this." He smiled. "I'm going to let go of one arm now, Ma'am, so we can talk. If you move to run or strike me, I will cuff you."

The police officer lifted one hand off Helen's right arm, eyeing her as he took his pad from his rear pocket.

"Hey, rookie," the hooded voice chimed in. "Mistake," the voice laughed, now closer and assuming the form of a very tall man, the gray hoodie pulled over the top of a forehead. Just visible under the edge of the hoodie, there was a ripple of reddish-blonde hair.

The officer watched Helen. He was holding her with one hand. She seemed distracted to him.

"You want to tell me why you assaulted that young woman?"

"She's not telling you nothing," the hooded voice laughed, his shadowy form twisting in imagined hilarity.

"I did not assault her," Helen said.

"I saw it, Ma'am."

"I was reaching for her arm."

"Ma'am, you had her arm. She was screaming and trying to pull her arm away from you."

A small crowd had gathered to see what was going on.

"That bitch is gonna win!" The voice in the hoodie turned into raucous laughter. Then his laughter boomed. "Just watch."

A truck's brakes screeched as a cab cut it off in the intersection.

The truck driver reached his head and finger out his window.

"Fuck you!" the cabbie cursed.

Helen suddenly closed her eyes tightly.

The cabbie leaned on his horn while he banged his other hand on the outside of his door.

The officer looked down to scribble a note on his pad, lifting his restraining hand off Helen.

At the corner, the light turned green, casting green light across the sign for Chinese take-out. The truck driver and cabbie honked back and forth furiously.

Helen opened her eyes, hauled her arm back, and with all her strength, hammered a tight right fist on the officer's chin with a slight upper thrust.

"What!!!" shouted the voice. "Score, bitch! Oh my, what a bitch!"

Looking around at his growing audience, the man in the hoodie was moving up and down as the voice within it grew riotous.

The police officer dropped, stone cold out, to the pavement.

"Just a lucky shot," someone in the audience shouted. "She just got lucky."

"No, sir! She's just badass," the slurred voice, gleeful with malice, shouted.

The group surrounding the voice applauded, and several other walkers stopped to ask what happened.

Helen had taken off running down Broadway at a ferocious pace, calling back "Sorry" in her wake.

She pulled every muscle into herself as she sped down Broadway, winding between couples, strollers, grocery carts and anything else in her way.

Far down the street, the screams of a different woman shrieked into the night like the screeching of a dying alley cat.

Two women in jogging gear looked at each other.

"Let's follow," one said to the other, and they took off running behind Helen.

The police officer came to, hoisted himself up on an elbow and called on his walkie-talkie for assistance. "What the fuck," he mumbled to himself. He scrambled up on his legs and ran behind the two women from the crowd.

The man in the hoodie trailed behind them at a slow trot. A wail of sirens from police cars rang through the air.

Two blocks ahead, as Helen roared by a vegetable stand, two city cop cars screeched to a halt, the cherry top still swirling. An officer threw the door open, ran after Helen, and grabbing her around her waist, threw her to the sidewalk.

Helen's face hit the pavement hard. She bled from the forehead.

The cop who had wrestled her down yanked her hands behind her back and cuffed her.

Helen lifted her head from the pavement, winced, and looked directly down Broadway. Her head swayed slightly as she held it up.

"Come on," the cop who had tackled her said. He pulled her to a standing position and dragged her toward the still wailing police car.

The two runners from the group came puffing up.

"Hey," they shouted. "Don't hurt her."

The cop kept his eyes straight.

The police officer Helen had decked limped into view, and the cop who had cuffed her stopped to let him approach as they talked.

She was arrested and read her Miranda rights.

The voice, the top half of his head deeply hidden by his gray hoodie, came limping up.

"Hey," he shouted. "She's hurt."

The officer who held Helen's arm turned.

"Stay back," he shouted.

"She was chasing another bitch who did something nasty to her," the voice explained to the small crowd around him.

Helen turned her head toward the voice.

"No," she said.

"What'd you say, lady?" the voice yelled, his arms gyrating.

"She didn't do anything," Helen said, barely audibly.

The voice shrugged his shoulders dramatically, holding his arms out.

"So then, why?"

"Yeah, who were you chasing?" the two women who'd run after Helen called out.

The police officer she'd knocked out said nothing but looked intently at her.

Helen dropped her head.

"Who was she?" the voice called out again, his arms outstretched in front of him, emphasizing the urgency of his question.

Helen tugged slightly against the cuffs that pinned her hands behind her back. She raised her head up and looked in the direction of the voice.

"My daughter," she said, dropping her jaw fully on her chest.

The officer who cuffed her pushed her head down slightly as she stepped into the car, and the car sped away.

The man inside the hoodie shook his head back and forth. "Terrible thing, mother chasing a daughter, daughter running away like that. Terrible thing." He took two heavy steps. He raised his right arm high in solidarity with Helen as his voice began to trail off. "Stay strong, my fine bitch. Stay strong." The hooded man mumbled on, but his voice faded away the further he got from the scene of arrest, and the faster he moved toward the liquor store at 84th and Broadway.

Chapter Two

The 19th Precinct edifice looked like the uneaten side of a wedding cake. The 1887 station house was stately and rococo at the same time. Once through the doors, the inside was not quite Brutalist style, but close. Areas were defined by royal blue metal tubing that climbed up door jambs heading toward nearby door jambs, but rather than descending, they zig zagged, penciling in larger areas before descending to the floor. Behind huge royal blue metal double doors, there was a long cold and clammy hallway that led to holding cells on either side. They were mostly individual cells, but the cell closest to the huge blue doors was meant to accommodate multiple guests.

That cell had typical black iron bars in the front and concrete walls in the back and on sides. No one could name their color. In places, they seemed white, but it was white that went to the thought of yellow in places. The floor spoke loudly. Painted gray a year or five years ago, it was scuffed with dirty marks, made by angry people who stomped into it with the toes of their shoes. Imprints of shoe soles marked the floor in patterns as if made for a space in an Escher painting. There were well over thirty old dried pieces of gum splattered on the floor, some looking dirty pink and others gone dark gray to the point that one wondered what kind of mold was growing in it. Five slats of flat metal bars, held together by brackets beneath them, formed a U around the sides and back of the cell to serve as a bench, which Helen had sat on for a few minutes before she stood up, looking out her cell bars.

Young officer Tucker, whom she knocked out, had gotten over his anger, and he decided not to press charges because he felt sorry for any woman who had to chase her own daughter, and he thought she was egged on by that drunk in the hoodie. This young officer was a softy, like a runny poached egg out of its shell, and within the year, it would go one way or the other with him. He'd either form a shell, or run out of the precinct headquarters and take up his uncle's offer to manage an uptown gas station.

In his empathy for Helen, he handed her the one piece of good luck she'd had in well over sixteen years. She got a rare Desk Appearance Ticket (DAT), which meant she would be released from the precinct house and not taken to Central Booking. She would be required to appear at a courthouse sometime later for arraignment on charges, and she still had to face charges of assaulting her daughter.

"Where's my lawyer?" Helen shouted, standing against the bars of the holding pen at the 19th precinct.

"I don't know," the fiftyish woman with a light brown face said. Her shoes clunked on the hallway floor as she swung a big royal blue door further open. Her short curly Afro surrounded a face with dark brown smiling eyes. She wore a blue uniform with a badge that read "19th Precinct." On the lapel of her jacket, there was a metal plaque that read "Olivia Klempton." An older man in uniform, his humpback so pronounced that it seemed he would topple over, thumped along after her. He carried a holstered gun and pushed himself against a wall to guard Officer Klempton.

"Well, you have to know," Helen said. She had been in this cell for what seemed like all night, but when she saw the officer's watch as her hand unlocked the holding pen, only forty-five minutes had passed since she made the call to her lawyer.

"Oh, do I have to know?" Officer Klempton said and walked over to the bench where an old dark brown woman in her seventies was stretched out snoring. She wore a loose cotton dress with little yellow flowers all over it, and she seemed cold.

"Miss Bertha," Olivia Klempton called to the old lady, "You okay?"

Miss Bertha rolled to her other side and faced the wall.

"Night, night, now," she murmured and continued snoring.

"Okay then," Klempton said and pulled the prison blanket up to Miss Bertha's chin.

Then Officer Klempton looked across the room where a twenty-something pale woman lay passed out on the opposite side of the room. She wore a yellow plaid Bergdorf spring coat, the back of her hand rested across her eyes, her elbow jutted out and moved up and down every time a shuddering snore came from reverberating lips.

Officer Klempton mumbled "two snoring yellow drunks" before walking over to the woman with the gray braid.

"You Ms. Helen Baird?" Olivia Klempton asked softly. "I'm here to verify some information Officer Tucker took."

"Who is Officer Tucker, and I really need someone to look at this gash in my forehead."

"Medics on the way, and Officer Tucker is the young officer you," Kempton lowered her voice to a whisper, and tried to suppress a little smile curling at the corners of her mouth, "tried to knee and then decked, Ms. Baird."

Helen couldn't suppress the chuckle in her throat.

Officer Klempton heard Helen's soft laughter and put the back of her hand fully over her mouth. Her chest rose and fell in rumbly laughter that started her coughing. A tall thin officer opened the blue door to the holding area and slowly walked past them. Officer Klempton allowed herself to come into a full cough before taking a tissue from her jacket, putting it over her mouth, and saying:

"My goodness! Pardon me." She winked at Helen, making Helen smile.

The tall thin officer went further down the hall, and the two women exchanged glances.

Helen whispered to Officer Klempton, "And that's why they're holding me here?"

"Uh-huh," Officer Klempton said. "They can't even talk upstairs; they're so riled up."

"Are they going to keep me here in this filthy cold place all night as pay back?"

"I heard that, too." Officer Klempton watched from the corner of her eye as the tall thin officer made his way back toward them. He turned his head to the old humpbacked officer with the gun in his holster.

"Look livelier, Bob," he said to the humpbacked officer.

Bob looked at him from under the rim of his cap as the tall thin officer opened one of the big blue doors and returned to where he'd come from.

"So, it's all night here?" Helen asked again, hoping for a different answer.

"See that long cabinet up near the ceiling?" Klempton asked.

"Yeah," Helen said, realizing she hadn't noticed it before.

"Lots and lots of warm blankets in there."

Helen made a low groan.

"I'm sorry, honey. I have no say in there." Officer Klempton tossed her head toward the big blue doors. "I just got to ask a lot of questions."

"Okay, shoot," Helen said. She looked over her shoulder to make sure Bob hadn't heard her.

Klempton suppressed laughter and winked at Helen. "Deaf, I think." She took out pad and pen, and said, "Now your name is Mrs. Helen Baird?"

"I'm a widow now," Helen said, turning away from Klempton. Helen could take toughness in others, but when someone was unexpectedly kind to her, she broke down.

Officer Klempton pursed her lips, "I'm so sorry about that."

Helen's eyes filled up like two tiny vases.

"Your date of birth? Take your time, honey."

"October 5, 1964," Helen said briskly, recovering herself.

"So, that makes you…"

"54," Helen said.

"You reside at 410 Tuttle Lane in Stanton Hall, New York?"

"Yes."

"How long you resided there, honey?"

"Twenty-eight years."

"You employed?"

"Yes."

"Where's that?"

"Editors for Hire in Sam Creek Falls, New York."

"And what do you do there?"

"I'm an editor."

Officer Klempton looked up from her pad and seemed to calculate something in her head.

"Got that. Your supervisor?"

"Sonia Glick. Do we have to notify her?"

"Don't have to, I don't think. Not my call, honey. I was just sent down with these questions."

"Now then. Why were you chasing the young woman?"

Helen teared up again. "I just wanted to talk to her. She's my daughter, and I thought if I could just talk a minute or two."

Officer Klempton looked at Helen from under her eyelids. "She's a runaway?" she asked in a low voice.

Helen glanced at Olivia Klempton briefly and turned away while nodding.

"I shouldn't have come into the City by myself," Helen said, shaking her head back and forth slowly. "Now Kristen knows I'm tracking her, and she'll hide. I didn't get to talk to her. All I did was tip her off to run further away. It was so stupid."

Officer Klempton tilted her head up and her eyes rolled up to the ceiling.

Helen stopped talking. Her head jerked toward Officer Klempton, and she laughed a few times. "You're thinking that wasn't the only stupid thing I did, right?"

"Why you say that?" Officer Klempton passed her hand over her mouth quickly.

Helen laughed again. "Well you aren't going to be the only one. Wait until Carmine hears about this."

"Carmine?" Officer Klempton scribbled her name on her pad.

"Sister Maria Carmelite, but we all call her Carmie," Helen said. "She's a nun."

"I got that," Officer Klempton said.

"She runs a support program for runaways and their families."

Officer Klempton nodded repeatedly as she scribbled all this down.

"She tells parents never to come in by ourselves to track down our kids. But that's hard, you know?"

"I'm sure it's very hard," Officer Klempton put her pad down near her knee and looked Helen directly in the eye.

"Do you have kids?" Helen asked.

"I have two sons," Officer Klempton's smile was from one mother to another.

Both women looked up at a commotion just outside the door to the holding area. The two big royal blue doors opened, and a gurney with medics at each end of it clambered toward the holding pen.

When they stopped near Helen's cell, they pulled a handle that stopped the gurney with a screech.

"Ms. Helen Baird," one of the medics called over to Helen.

"Yes."

"We're here to assist you."

Officer Klempton squeezed her eyes slightly in acknowledgement of the medics' higher priority business with Helen.

"I'll try to come back later," she smiled at Helen, "if they want any more information."

"Try to come back." Helen smiled.

Officer Klempton took the tips of Helen's fingers and gently shook them back and forth. "I will," she said and walked toward the big royal blue doors as the medics crowded into Helen's cell with their equipment.

Within fifteen minutes the medics had cleaned and bandaged Helen's forehead, both agreeing that stitches weren't necessary.

After the medics left, Helen just stared down the hall. She stared at the huge royal blue doors that separated those who would spend the night in cells from those who would keep them there. She figured it to be after midnight and wondered if anyone else would be coming through those doors tonight. A loudspeaker announced lights would be dimmed for sleep in two minutes. Helen had reconciled herself to a night in jail, but she had no idea what she'd do all night. She knew she would not sleep. She figured she had five or six hours to pass in this cold cell.

"Now I'm a criminal?" she mumbled. "How did that happen?" She thought of her brother, Paul, in jail since he was nineteen, convicted of murdering a man who owed him $5000. Helen hadn't seen him in over twenty-five years, and she imagined he'd been framed for the murder. "Falsely accused and jailed," Helen said to herself, "just like me." She rested her head against the black iron rails of the cell.

"Never heard so much mumbling," a voice behind Helen spoke.

Helen whirled around and came face to face with Miss Bertha, bracing herself on one elbow from her bench bed. She peered at Helen from a toothless face.

"Hi," Helen said. "I thought you were sleeping."

"Was," Miss Bertha said, "but no more." Miss Bertha reached under the skirt of her yellow-flowered dress and pulled a pint of Canadian blended whisky out from under the waistband.

"Like a drink?" She smiled.

"How can you?" Helen whispered.

"Oh, honey, I'm in here most nights. The kind of frisking they do on me these days is touch my knees, pat my shoulders and head, but all the in between they just leave well enough alone. There's times they just wave me on through."

Helen looked at Miss Bertha's pint bottle. "We don't have glasses."

"Nope, but we got swigs. You looking troubled."

"I am," Helen said. "Okay, give me a swig. Please."

Miss Bertha handed over the pint bottle, and Helen took a large gulp.

"It's very nice of you to share," Helen said, wiping her mouth with her sleeve.

"Most folk don't talk to me, you know," Miss Bertha said matter-of-factly.

"Why not?" Helen asked.

"I'm too old to talk to!" Miss Bertha howled.

Helen put her finger to her lips. "They'll hear and come down here."

Miss Bertha shook her head slowly. Her pointer finger made a circular motion indicating the whole area they were in. "Sound proof," she whispered.

"Oh," Helen said.

"So, you go on and talk to me," Miss Bertha said. "I can tell you got things on your mind, and I like when people talk to me."

Helen passed the pint bottle to Miss Bertha, and she took a long swig and lay down on the bench bed. "Just start with why you in here."

"Well, I was chasing my daughter," Helen began.

"Why you do that?"

"She's a runaway."

"How she get that way?" Miss Bertha asked.

"It's a long story, Miss Bertha."

"And we got whisky to swig on." Miss Bertha laughed.

"I'll start when Kristen, that's my daughter's name, oh, and I'm Helen," Helen reached over her hand to Miss. Bertha.

"Pleased," was all Miss Bertha said. "Go on. You said, when Kristen, so go on."

"When Kristen was in Sixth grade."

"And then," Miss Bertha's voice was slightly slurry as she reached for another swig from the bottle. She passed the bottle to Helen.

"Well, sixth grade was a great year, the last good year," Helen began. She kept up her story for about five minutes until Miss Bertha's mouth erupted with a honking snore.

Helen smiled and thought about trying to sleep herself, but her story was in her head now. She moved down to the end of Miss Bertha's bench, leaned against the wall, bent her knees and pulled her feet close to her body. All evening, the phrase 'I'm a criminal now' had been stuck right at the level of her diaphragm. She decided to think her way through this mess of how she became a criminal.

***

The backyard was like a stage the summer after Kristen's Sixth grade. Oaks and maples in a semi-circle far from the house formed the backdrop of the deep, wide meadow. Five running girls between eleven and twelve chased each other, or was it the warm May breeze chasing them as they ran with their windmills and bright red, yellow, and blue kites on short sticks. The circles they ran in were fueled by laughter, a hearty cook-out lunch followed by s'mores over the fire pit, and candy they thought they had "stolen" from one of Helen's kitchen drawers. In fact, she re-stocked her drawers every day with mints, Good and Plenty, and gum drops.

As the girls dropped on the rye grass to laugh some more, Helen watched them from the kitchen window and thought it was as if they were lying on a grass blanket. One or two rested on an elbow and looked toward the oak and maple arc at the back of the meadow. It had seemed an opaque curtain until sunlight pierced through it, making it a transparent scrim. The girls might have seen behind that scrim a doe or two and new born fawns scampering along trails they were just then making through the woods.

The five girls, who had ruled their elementary school, had seemed unusually reflective on graduation day a few weeks before. Their mothers, all friends now, were used to seeing this bunch of girls travel around all together, like grapes on a stalk. The mothers hadn't yet recognized how uneasy they felt seeing the girls develop at different rates, no longer like grapes, but more like cucumbers on a vine, some enlarging quickly while others remained slight. Only two, Jen and Nicky, the two athletes, were justifiably in bras, but the others were in concave starter bras. It was Paula's mother who defined something they were all seeing. At graduation, she'd leaned over to whisper to Helen, "They're all terrified of next year. The new school and being babies in it all over again."

Of course! That was it. Of all the mothers, Helen was particularly discomfited by inevitable looming changes in the group. Kristen was an only child, and she had lured herself into thinking this group would always surround her daughter and make up for Kristen's lack of siblings.

Helen vowed on the spot to let Kristen have a summer of childhood where she could sop up all the joys of a child's freedom before she headed for the trenches of seventh grade at Miller Junior High School. Helen downplayed any preparation for the following September, didn't even bring up new fall clothes for Kristen. Instead, she bought several cotton bedspreads that she spread on their meadow. She encouraged Kristen to have her group over for picnics and overnights in a huge tent Helen bought and put up in a spot she could see from her bedroom window. She had her husband, Hank, make a clearing near the entrance to the woods so the girls could have adventures in the closer parts of the woods. There, the girls found a trail, which they ran through with their kites, screaming that something in their collective imagination was on fire. Then they'd flop down on the lawn, stretch, and roll toward one another with their secrets. Helen looked out her kitchen window as often as she could and think *our lawn is a grass blanket for them to rest on.* If it was the end of childhood, it should be an ending as close to a modern Walden as she could make it.

The first weeks of seventh grade were hard on Kristen and Helen. Predictably, Kristen hated it. She knew no one in her classes, and the girls from the Morrow School were so mean. They were bigger, more developed, and more sophisticated than the girls in Kristen's group. The Morrow girls all had at least small bust lines, and many of them had older brothers whose parties they had attended for years.

"Yeah, and this one girl, Sarah Brambel, told Paula that she drinks beers at her brother's parties." Kristen was full of disdain for Sarah Brambel, but Helen noted that Paula, always the most outgoing one in the group, had evidently found a way to have a conversation with this Sarah, who sounded to Helen like the most popular girl in the new Seventh grade class.

Helen heard Kristen's complaints, ones that were echoed by Sheila's mother, but not the other mothers. *Sheila and Kristen, always the more timid ones in their group, would take longer to adjust,* Helen thought. All the mothers girded for a difficult year, and they commiserated with one another when one girl went on a crying jag or behaved sullenly for what seemed like weeks on end. Jen's mother said she planned to move out of her house because Jen had suddenly turned ornery and had screamed "I hate you" at her more than once. Each of the girls was having a hard time adjusting to Miller Jr. High, but Helen feared that Kristen was more distressed and sullen than any of them.

Near Halloween, the school held a special Seventh Grade dance, but Kristen didn't want to go. When Helen suggested she give it a try, Kristen screamed at her, "Yeah, and stand there like a cow near the wall all night? Thanks, Mom!" Neither Sheila nor Nicky would go. "Not even considering it." Nicky's mother reported her daughter's plans about the dance. But Jen and Paula were excited to be going, and Helen felt what other mothers were feeling, that their girls' group would now fracture, some going one way and some the other. Sheila's mother decided on therapy to help Sheila adjust, and Helen was interested in exploring the idea, but Hank was solidly against it.

"What, and stigmatize her as a kid who needs a shrink? For God's sake, give her a year or two to get used to the new school, all the hormonal changes, and just plain growing up. Who said it would be easy? She's got to toughen up a little."

Helen agreed to let Kristen have that year to find her feet without turning to therapy.

By the time the Eighth Grade Christmas Dance came, all the girls in the old group, but Kristen and Sheila, were thrilled to be going. Helen worried about why it was taking Kristen and Sheila so long to adjust. Hank again said to leave her alone, that she and Sheila would come out of their shells when they were good and ready.

Helen might not have listened to Hank so readily if he'd been a remote father, but he had always been active in Kristen's life. He was there when Kristen was born. She had watched Hank diaper Kristen, take her on walks around the block, Kristen's diaper waddling under her short dress. Helen had seen Hank try to teach Kristen to swing at a baseball, hit a tennis ball, and even throw a football. She'd watched him stay up nights working with Kristen over her math problems, reading her English papers, and boring her to death with his stories about history. The only time in Kristen's life that Hank took a few steps back from her was when Kristen's breasts finally started developing, and Helen knew it was because he didn't want to take any chance of giving Kristen the slightest self-consciousness about her body.

By the ninth grade, when even Sheila had joined the others in mall outings and at a ninth-grade graduation dance, Helen insisted it was time to take Kristen to a therapist. She was the only one in her group who hadn't ever successfully transitioned into junior high school, and now high school was around the bend. Even more worrying, in the last year she'd gotten lethargic, and sometimes she was so spacey Helen lost her temper with her. Kristen had a mobile phone by then, which Helen had gotten her for safety, and Kristen had misplaced two of them. "I don't know where I put it," she'd scream at Helen until Helen just bought her another. The summer after ninth grade, Kristen slept an inordinate amount, and after ruling out mono during Kristen's appointment at the Children's Center, Helen concluded that Kristen was clinically depressed. There was no other explanation. Dr. Barnes, whom Kristen saw for annual check-ups and whenever she didn't feel well, had never found any reason to order elaborate tests. He checked her thoroughly, ran some minimal tests, and found her normal for her age. The answer had to be psychological. Helen knew Hank would disapprove, so she didn't tell him that Kristen was seeing a therapist, committed to bi-monthly appointments. After the initial intake, the therapist found nothing extreme in Kristen's condition but most likely underlying anxiety for which she was prescribed medication. The therapist suggested the anxiety probably made Kristin have a difficult time adjusting, not so much to junior high school because after all now that was a known environment, but more likely to the on-going changes in her body. Helen, who was keen to keep the therapy from Hank, said nothing to anyone about it. She guarded the secrecy of the appointments by throwing decoys at Hank if need be.

"Oh, I'm taking Kristen to get a new T-shirt she mentioned."

Helen and Hank had never lied to one another, so she was not confident that some small odd inflection in her voice wasn't betraying her all along.

A day came when Kristen left her medication in the kitchen after she'd taken a pill with milk, and Hank found the pill bottle next to the electric can opener.

He and Helen had never screamed at each other, but they did that day.

"What the hell, Helen? What the hell? You actually went behind my back to send my daughter to a shrink and permitted her to take medication without informing me?"

"Well you are just behind the times," Helen screamed back. "Kids who don't adjust see therapists. That's just how it happens!"

"No, that is not just how it happens, Helen! How it happens is that two parents who trust each other sit down and talk these things through and come to a mutual decision. That's how it happens, or I should say, how it should happen! But no, you just went off on your own, forgetting this is my daughter, too!"

They stopped yelling because Kristen ran down the stairs, crying that they were screaming. Hank didn't acknowledge or talk to Helen for two days. She finally sidled up to him in the kitchen.

"Come on, Hankie. This is for Kristen's good."

Hank just looked at Helen, and said, "You know, Helen, it's a big price we've paid for this even if you are right, which I doubt."

"Oh, you are just so stubborn, Hank."

"Stubborn? You think this is about being stubborn? What if this is about I've lost a lot of faith in you. I don't entirely trust you now, and I sure as hell don't see myself being on your team! There is no team between us. You've destroyed that, Helen."

Hank said nothing more to Helen about it, and nothing about Kristen's going to therapy, but a coolness had grown between them, and neither seemed able to recover the spontaneous warmth that had always been between them.

After six months of Kristen's therapy, Helen had to admit she saw no improvement in Kristen, so she found a new therapist. Both Helen and Hank were worried silly when Kristen complained of mysterious pains that went from her shoulders to her knees, and that she sometimes appeared to walk stiffly, and, on weekends, she seemed almost catatonic. Hank talked about his worries, but Helen didn't because by now she was enthralled with the new therapist, Dr. Thomas, and trusted her treatment plan for Kristen. Dr. Thomas felt that Kristen had a deeply troubling memory or memories, probably something she had misunderstood in early childhood, and that she and Kristen were on a journey to discover what was buried in her. Once discovered, it could be dispelled. The peeling of the onion, she called it. She felt that within the next six months to a year, she and Kristen would arrive at the core memory or memories causing Kristen to sabotage her growth.

It took Helen six months to sit Hank down and tell him about Dr. Thomas and her ideas about what was holding Kristen back in her life.

Hank said nothing, and when Helen asked him why he had nothing to say, he responded:

"Because we're no longer a team, Helen, like I told you. I no longer trust you to pay the slightest attention to my views about Kristen's health, so, go ahead with your therapy, but I'm telling you now, Helen, that if I see further deterioration in Kristen, I'm taking charge, and don't expect me to seek your counsel."

Helen left the room in a huff.

She knew their relationship had been damaged. They weren't having sex at all during this time, but she believed strongly that she and Dr. Thomas were right about Kristen's treatment. She had to put her relationship with Hank second to guarding Kristen's healing.

What are you supposed to do when the life of a child is at stake? she'd say to herself when she became alarmed about the coldness that had settled between Hank and her.

After six months of Dr. Thomas's treatment, Hank walked into the kitchen and stood, arms folded across his stomach, in front of Helen.

"So, where's this progress you and Dr. Thomas speak so highly of," he said to Helen. "I want to take her to old Doc. Jenkins."

"No, Hank," Helen whined. "We haven't given Dr. Thomas the time she's asked for to get to Kristen's core troubling memories. They are making progress."

"Yeah, that's what Dr. Thomas tells you and you tell yourself, Helen. The kid is not getting better. She's hurting. Just look at her face."

"I'm not going to argue with you, Hank. We just need to give Dr. Thomas time to unravel whatever is buried inside Kristen's troubled mind."

"So, 'I'm not going to argue with you, Hank' means that you are right, and I am wrong, and what I think as her father does not even bear considering. Is that it, Helen?"

Helen looked Hank dead in the eyes.

"Well, if you want to put it that way."

"Damn it, Helen. Let her continue this voodoo therapy that you insist on, but let her also be checked out physically. I have had the greatest trust in Dr. Jenkins for over twenty-five years. Remember he has been my doctor for years now."

"And sometime down the line, okay," Helen said. "Just not now. Kristen sees Dr. Barnes if anything bothers her. You know that."

"He's a quack. And things are bothering Kristen. What about all this pain and stiffness she's having?"

"Look, Hank. Dr. Thomas needs Kristen's full attention now, and I don't want Kristen side-tracked by someone finding some minor issue—she needs Vitamin B Complex or something like that—which might give Kristen an excuse for her behavior rather than facing the deeper underlying issues she evidently has."

"Okay. I'm not going to argue with you any more, Helen."

"What does that mean, Hank?"

"It means I am her father, Helen."

When Kristen remained lethargic and continued to complain about chronic pain.

Hank simply made the appointment with Dr. Jenkins for the same time Helen had a long work meeting scheduled, and he took Kristen to him. Dr. Jenkins right away suspected Stage III Lyme disease and told Hank to take Kristen to the Mayo Clinic for a work up. He said Mayo was on the cutting edge then of dealing with untreated Lyme disease. Hank looked through Helen's calendar to discover when she'd be in meetings in the next weeks, contacted Mayo to schedule tests for Kristen, canceled his jobs for that time and booked flights for himself and Kristen. He also booked a flight for Helen, but not until two days after he and Kristen arrived in Rochester, Minnesota. He would make sure Helen was at Mayo with them when they received results, but he would no longer permit her to block medical testing.

He struggled over his next action, but he saw no option. He was sure when Helen found out he and Kristen were in Rochester, she'd fly right out to join them. Then she'd cancel the tests he'd set up, arguing that Kristen's time with her therapist was sacrosanct. He was so certain about this scenario that he went into Helen's purse, left on her dresser while she took her shower the morning he and Kristen were to leave for Mayo. He took her credit cards and bank cards. He'd call her as soon as they landed in Rochester, and let her know he'd taken the cards but that she had a ticket in the top drawer of his dresser for a flight leaving in two days. Short of borrowing money, she couldn't get to Rochester in time to block the tests Kristen so badly needed. He hoped, but did not believe, that she would be rational and understand that as Kristen's father, he could no longer permit Dr. Thomas and Helen to forestall physical testing of Kristen, whether it interrupted Dr. Thomas's work with Kristen or not.

When Helen returned home from her meeting and found that Kristen was not at home, she went into a panic. She called Dr. Thomas, but couldn't reach her right away. She called the houses of Kristen's old friends, but none had seen Kristen recently. Only after an hour, she called Hank.

"Do you know where Kristen is," she asked coldly.

"Yes, I do. She's right here with me."

He told her they were at Mayo because Dr. Jenkins strongly suspected advanced Lyme's Disease caused by an initial tick bite followed by lack of treatment. He explained Dr. Jenkins had urged Hank to take Kristen to Mayo for testing that would confirm Lyme's Disease or not and discover whether, after all these years of progression, treatment could help Kristen.

"I am flying out there, Hank."

"Yes. I bought you a ticket. It's for Thursday. Look, Helen, you've blocked everything I'm trying to do for Kristen. She's my child, too, and she's sick. She's physically sick, and I can't have you flying here and taking her home for more therapy before these tests are done. She needs a thorough set of testing, and she'll get it. I've told the doctors we won't get a single result until you are in the room with us. But I will not permit you to block these tests, and for that reason, I've taken your credit cards and bank cards."

"What!!" Helen screeched.

"I hope we can work this out, Helen. But later."

Livid, Helen hung up.

When Helen got to Mayo two days later, she found Hank in a waiting room while Kristen was just finishing her final tests. Although Hank was not that happy to see Helen take the seat beside him, his mind was too absorbed with the coming test results to feel anger toward her. He looked at her and said:

"They said they'll know some answers in a few hours. I told them we'd meet to review tests tomorrow, in case your flight got delayed today. Let me go tell the coordinator that we'll meet them later today as soon as they know something."

Helen nodded, and Hank rushed out of the waiting room.

Both were surprised there was no outward recrimination between them. They were each exhausted, but they also sensed that they would not have energy for a battle between them because they were entering a far more formidable battle, one that would make the squabbles between them moot.

Their meeting later that afternoon confirmed they had entered new territory, a place of no return. Although no serologic abnormalities were found, silver staining detected spirochetes in Kristen's tissues, and based on the test that targets a DNA sequence specific to Lyme Disease, doctors could determine *borrelia burgdorferi* in Kristen's system.

In later weeks, after two more trips to Mayo, they were gently guided through the literature on the psychiatric effects of untreated Stage III, or chronic Lyme borreliosis. Although Kristen was immediately put on a course of antibiotics, Dr. Patel, the soft-spoken, very bright and unfailingly empathetic doctor who worked with them, told them plainly that they had only very guarded hope that antibiotics would affect the borreliosis. Their team had reached a conclusion, based on physical tests and clinical observation that Kristen's Stage III Lyme Disease had resulted in what was a severe psychiatric syndrome known as organic psychosis, and that such psychosis was irreversible at the stage it was seen in Kristen. They could offer no prognosis.

It was a final verdict for Hank and Helen, and a frail coat of normalcy split, exposing beneath it, chaotic oceans of sorrow, and Helen and Hank knew the end of life as they had known it.

***

Miss Bertha stretched in her sleep, and her leg hit Helen's leg, jarring the memories out of Helen's head. She heard the sound of a horn echoing from the streets outside. In a minute there were two more horns. She heard a thump from somewhere behind the big metal doors. It must be very early morning. Helen looked over at Miss Bertha.

"You like my story, Miss Bertha?"

"Huh?" Miss Bertha turned over. "What. What'd I miss?"

"You didn't miss anything," Helen said.

"I did, I know I did," Miss Bertha was struggling to stay awake. "Start over," she said.

Helen laughed. "Okay, but you stay awake, and I'll tell you the story of why Miss Helen became a criminal."

"This a good one," Miss Bertha said, and turned facing the wall.

Chapter Three

Helen's lawyer had her released by 7 a.m., and she was home in her expanded farmhouse an hour north of the City by 10 a.m. She left a message for Carmie at the convent, confessing that she had broken Carmie's cardinal rule. Carmie would make her pay for her bit of hubris.

Helen just had time to change. Last week, she'd invited a woman whose daughter had recently run away to come by for coffee this morning to give her support. Throwing on a clean blouse, Helen put on lipstick and ran down to answer the door bell.

***

Five miles away, Sister Maria Carmelite made a hard left in the orange and white 1968 VW German Kombi bus her old mother had bought her. "Think I'll spin by Helen's house." She turned up her radio, blaring Sinatra's "Fly Me to the Moon."

Carmie's mother gave her the bus so she could get out of the convent more. Now with her bus, Carmie had something to do when she was off duty. She could ditch her nun clothes for dungarees and stretched-out sweaters for long rides in these rural farmlands. Rolling hills, ambling twists in the road, huge elms and spruce weaving through the oaks heartened Carmie, and she loved yellow spring in early May when forsythia and daffodils sprawled through the countryside.

Carmie had her radio top-volume as she let her voice enhance Sinatra's *Let me play among the stars.* When she got to Tuttle Lane, she slowed and turned the radio down for the mile drive under a majestic canopy of ancient arched black maples.

Helen's old expanded white farm house would be coming up on the right. Set close to the road, its large custom windows on either side of the front door glistened in the sunlight. On the left, a long bank of wide kitchen windows gave mutual visibility between the street and kitchen.

Carmie spotted a car she didn't immediately recognize in Helen's driveway and slowed further to look at the license plate.

"What the hell!" Carmie yelled as she stopped the bus. She did recognize this car, after all, because the day before, it was parked beside her bus during her meeting with its owner, Janet Masland, whose sixteen-year-old daughter had run away. Carmie's mission, working with runaways and their families, brought Janet to her office, and after, Carmie had walked her out and seen Janet get into this car.

"So, doing my job, are you, Helen?" Carmie rolled by Helen's front door muttering, "Eight years looking for your daughter does not make you an expert, Helen!" As Carmie passed the huge kitchen windows, she spotted a white blur entering the kitchen. She sped beyond the rambling farm house on its four acres of green meadow which receded into deep woods.

***

Helen, her long gray single braid down the back of her white blouse, stood at her kitchen island. pouring coffee for her guest, waiting in the adjoining sitting room. Helen inhaled her fresh-ground coffee. The newly met young Janet Masland, just forty-two, a normally attractive, petite, dirty blonde, was now crying, weeping, and sobbing between gasps, lost, desolate, desperate, inconsolable over her daughter, Lindsay, running away weeks earlier.

Helen put two piping hot coffee cups on a tray just as a sharp glint passed through the kitchen windows. Looking up, Helen saw the familiar faded orange and white VW bus roll slowly by. She called out to herself, "Carmie? What the hell!" The bus sped away.

Not wanting to leave Janet alone for long, Helen held the tray in one hand, and stuck a small Kleenex box under her arm. "Honest to God, that nun thinks everyone else in that convent is the problem. Helen addressed the tray as Carmie. Well, no, Carmie! Problem is YOU!"

Helen rushed back up the three slate steps to her sitting room off the kitchen.

Tears filled Janet's eyes, but she was looking out the expansive farmhouse style windows Hank, Helen's late husband, had installed across the back of the first floor.

"It's really beautiful here," Janet said. She whispered, "thanks," taking the Kleenex box.

"It is," Helen answered, the corners of her mouth turning up at the sight of her tallest willow.

"Can Carmie really help?" Janet asked, sniffing.

"What else do we have, Janet?"

"They can't keep moving around on the streets forever, can they," Janet asked plaintively.

"They don't. Extended families and friends in the City let groups of kids stay with them for weeks at a time—kids, I say, but mine isn't a kid anymore. She's twenty-seven now. Do you have any idea where Lindsay is?"

"The City. I think."

"Carmie may get you a clue when she goes in next."

Janet stopped sniffing and looked up, suddenly. Helen, seeing this change in Janet's mood, turned toward her.

"I heard Sister Carmie has a glass eye. Is that true?"

"Yeah, she does. Lost her eye while on the run."

Janet cocked her head.

"She was a runaway herself."

"No way!"

"Yup. She tells her story in the second group support meeting."

"Tell me!" Janet shifted her body to face Helen.

"Well, I shouldn't steal her thunder, but the way she tells it, Carmie's mother was appalled by the birth process and wanted nothing to do with more children and not much to do with the one she had. Now they're close, but not while Carmie was growing up. Her mother worked—don't know what she did—and she wasn't home much, so Carmie was raised by a lady up the street who watched her. When her mother was home, she always had a dime-store romance novel in her hand. She put a hassock in the laundry room, and she'd sneak off to read and smoke cigarettes in there."

"Oh, Jeez. How sad."

"Sadder because Carmie's father left when she was three. No one was watching her. When she turned thirteen, she started sleeping with a boy in her apartment building. She climbed out her window at night, went up her fire escape, ran across the roof and down this guy's fire escape to his room. Sex all night. I guess nobody told her you can get pregnant from sex, so when she got pregnant, she was flabbergasted, but the boy knew about a clinic, and Carmie got an abortion. When her mother found out, she freaked and hit Carmie on the head with her latest novel. Then she padlocked the window in Carmie's room."

"Sounds like a horrible mother."

"Yeah, wonder what our kids say."

Janet's face screwed up, ready to cry.

Helen patted her hand again and said, "Anyway."

Janet looked up.

"Carmie broke her bedroom window, but this time, she climbed down. Then she jumped about fifteen feet to the pavement. She says she loved how her feet tingled when she jumped because it meant she was free. She tells how she ran down her street to the subway and walked back and forth on the platform until a subway came and took her to the streets of Manhattan."

"My God," Janet said. "What a story."

"There's more," Helen said. She abruptly turned her head toward the front window.

"What is it?" Janet asked.

"Hear that thunder? I think a storm is coming."

"Oh, well I'll have to wait till it's over to leave, so go on," Janet said.

"Well I really should let Carmie tell this," Helen hesitated.

"You can't leave me hanging now."

"Yeah, okay. So, Carmie went home to her mother after five years. She'd been raped twice, beaten-up three times, and hospitalized once. That's when she lost her eye. It was too damaged from a beating for doctors to save."

"Which eye?"

"Left. The left one. You can tell when she's talking to you. The other eye moves, but the left one just sort of stares at you."

"Oh, God! Go on."

"Well, Carmie says when her mother saw the black patch over her eye, she tried to lift it, but Carmie pushed her hand down and told her to stop, that she was getting a glass eye from a clinic she knew. Her mother asked her if they'd be the same color. Her eyes."

"Oh, my God."

"Yeah, but something nice came out of it because then Carmie and her mother sat at the kitchen table and had a cup of tea together, and that's when Carmie told her mother she was joining the Pallottine Sisters, and her mission would be to develop programs to help the county's growing number of runaways and their families. Towns like ours with railroads that go into Manhattan have a real problem with runaways these days. Carmie asked if she could live with her mother until she got her glass eye and joined the order. She says her mother grabbed her hand from across the table, and kept saying *I love you. I love you.*"

"Whoa," Janet said.

"Yeah, and now Carmie is very close to her mother."

"Oh, that ends wonderful!"

"Does it?" Helen asked.

Janet sat still for a moment. Then her eyes welled up again.

"How can you love a child who doesn't want to know you?"

"Oh, Janet. I've asked that so many times."

"But why?" Janet wailed. "Why should we have to ask that? I just want to die," Janet could barely be heard beneath howling sobs.

Five minutes later, Janet's wave of grief had run its course. She was calm and quiet.

Helen looked out the window to see if a storm had just gone by.

Janet fumbled in her purse for her phone.

"Wow, already one o'clock! I need to get going." Janet stood up. "Thank you so much, Helen. It won't last, but I feel better right now."

"Good," Helen said, walking Janet to the front door. "Call any time, and see you tonight at the first support group meeting. St. Mary's at 7 p.m."

"I hope that will be a help," Janet said.

"Oh, yes. A big help," Helen echoed, smiled at Janet again, and watched her go down the front porch steps.

***

After passing Helen's house earlier, Carmie drove fast down Tuttle Lane into town, slamming her brakes at the stop sign. She yanked her steering wheel right so fast that her hand knocked off the pewter Ave Maria pin a priest had given her years ago.

She reached around her feet for the pin.

"Crap," she yelled, when her rambling hand pushed it under her seat.

Continuing along a country road to the convent in Nashett, N.Y. Carmie let herself guess how much weight Helen had gained in recent months.

Carmie pulled into the parking area for the Community of St. Mary's. She was glad to see that none of the other nuns had taken her parking spot and was hoping she wouldn't run into any of them in the kitchen while grabbing lunch.

She ate a grilled American cheese sandwich and was steeping her tea.

"Don't forget to clean the toaster-oven," Sister Rosalie, a fat nun with eyes that seemed to rove involuntarily in circles, exclaimed. She turned to leave.

"You bet," Carmie said, an edge in her voice.

Sister Rosalie turned back swiftly and stood at the kitchen door, looking at Carmie but saying nothing. When Carmie didn't look up, Sister Rosalie left.

Five minutes later as Carmie lingered over her tea, Sister Rosalie popped her head around the corner of the entry door and stared at Carmie.

"What, Sister? What's on your mind? Oh, the toaster oven. You got it, Sister."

Carmie took a wad of paper towels from the roll, bunched them up and passed them furiously around the bottom of the toaster oven, wadded them tighter, turned and smiled at Sister Rosalie. She bashed them into the garbage can as if she were a pro basketball star in the NBA.

Chapter Four

After Janet left, Helen, tired from her ordeal at the 19th precinct, lay on her sofa in the sitting room, gazing out the huge window that was nearly the full back wall of this room. She stared at her garden thinking that her life hadn't been going well for the last several years.

Dumpster, her large gray shorthair cat, jumped onto her lap.

Helen groaned with the weight of him on her legs, and adjusted him so he lay down. She stroked his neck and then took his head in her hands.

"Lately, it's just bumper cars for me, Dumpy. I wake up and jerk into high-gear. I make lists for the grocery store and the hardware store, but then my foot slips off the pedal, and I jerk to a stop and get slammed from behind by some memory that just about paralyzes me."

The cat paused his grooming for a second and looked at her, his hind leg straight in the air like an instrument he was playing.

"Oh, so you want me to talk to you while you groom, do you? Okay. Well here is what I have to say. I know what to do, Dumpy. All these years of therapy, and I know what to do."

The cat kept washing a side of his paw to use as a washcloth around his whiskers.

"I have to keep my thoughts on myself. That is what the therapist keeps saying. I have to be like you, Dumpster. You are always thinking about you, right? The cat kept washing his face with his paws. I have to be more like you!"

Dumpster walked down to her knees, turned twice and then nuzzled himself between her lower legs for a nap in the sun.

Lying still, she again gazed out the window at her garden. She saw movement further out. Two newborn fawns were scampering across a trail that led into the woods. They leapt after one another in a crisscross pattern that made Helen think of the plaits of a braid, winding across one another to their wispy ends. Her eyes filled with the image of her daughter's tangled brown hair, thin and wispy, streaming across her back as she fled her mother's clutch at the corner of 84th and Broadway the night before. Helen's hands still knew the weight of that hair when it was healthy in Sixth grade as she plaited it into a French braid down Kristen's back. She had the scent of that hair in her nostrils, and the feel and weight of it in her hands for all time.

She sat up abruptly. Dumpster, disturbed, looked at her.

"Probably shouldn't be thinking this," she complained to Dumpster.

He jumped away from her legs and went to a rocking chair closer to the window. He jumped up and circled the braided chair pad until he found the right spot.

Helen snuggled deeper into the couch. She didn't know what to do when these memories with a long shadow came. Should she let them linger or chase them out? It was almost impossible to chase them out.

She kept asking herself what she had in life, and the answer that came back was she had questions about her life that she'd never asked before.

Her childhood had been idyllic to a point, but ultimately it had made her a skeptic.

Most people thought her parents, Harold and Eva Baird, perfect, and Helen had always thought they were perfect, too.

Harold Baird, a professor of geology at The University of Hartford, commuted to his graduate classes three days a week. On weekends, he took Helen on long walks in the woods and told her about rock formations they passed. Helen never thought rocks were that important and always wanted to tell her father, it's humans that are important, but after a walk with him, she wondered if maybe he was right.

Eva Baird was a first-rate volunteer. She was Helen's class mother for all but two years when another mother finally beat her out. Theirs was, Helen felt, a perfect family until her brother, Paul, was born seven years after her.

Even as a newborn, there was something about how his hair fell that made Paul look like a hoodlum. At three, he'd grab the tails of goldfish their father had won at a carnival, take them out of their bowl and swing them around and around until someone stopped him. In third grade, he hung out with fifth graders who shot arrows into trees until they saw a pack of stray dogs and shot the arrows into the sides of the dogs. Paul claimed he only shot trees, and it was the older boys who shot the dogs, but Helen didn't know if she believed him. In eighth grade, he went next door to "borrow" money from the old lady who lived there. When she surprised him by walking into the room he was snooping in, he hit her in the stomach. Just after he graduated from high school, he was arrested for murder and sent to prison for thirty years. Police said he killed a man who owed him $5000. Helen never knew if the man owed Paul money or whether Paul killed him, but since then, she hadn't seen him or even thought about him often because she didn't think she wanted to know him. She concluded that if you can be almost perfect but have a bad brother, then there is nothing predictable in life.

But this day a startling thought came to her: she had, in fact, abandoned Paul. Where was he? Was he even alive? Why hadn't she kept in touch with Paul, who might have changed? Why couldn't she love him as a brother even if he was flawed? She judged him, but maybe she had failed to judge herself. Maybe she wasn't the nice person she thought she was. Had she made herself up? She'd always said she valued family and friends, yet here it was in front of her. Paul was family, and she'd thrown him away. And Kristen couldn't bear to be near her. Helen's heart stung, as it always did, at the knowledge that she had been responsible for Kristen's devastating disease. She had accused Hank of being stubborn in insisting that Kristen see a doctor whose study was the physical body, but she was the one who was stubborn. She had insisted on only one way of treating Kristen. She had been wrong. Just plain wrong. Kristen had every reason to hold her responsible for the disintegration of her life. The lines between who Helen thought she was and who she might be were like blurred letters on a rain-soaked envelope.

Chapter Five

Helen had to drag herself off her sofa because she was meeting her boss, Sonia Glick, for an early dinner at *Sonata*, a restaurant new to Helen, to discuss her next assignment. *Sonata* was Sonia's pick because it served farm fresh food, but it was forty miles away.

Sonia Glick, the Lead Editor at *Editors for Hire*, managed thirty-five freelance editors who got their assignments from and reported to her. *Editors for Hire*, on the Rockland County outskirts of Manhattan, was an eighteen-year-old company owned by two disinterested but prominent county lawyers. Spencer Samuelson, a heavy-set man resembling an accountant who should be wearing a green plastic visor. The company had been more lucrative than he'd expected, and it grew a reputation among Manhattan writers and publishers as the little diamond just outside the City, its editors in high demand. When Samuelson founded the law firm, Samuelson & Arshen with Dick Arshen, part of the deal was that Arshen got shares in *Editors for Hire* because he liked to tell clients he was invested in the arts. If Samuelson could be said to resemble an accountant, Dick Arshen was more like a prowling lion on the savannah. Together they made an invincible team from the time they first set up as cronies in law. Their goal was to gain influence in county politics, starting in the eastern part of the county where they first established their firm and spreading into the south-western end of the county. The two were like a Sunday couple on a tandem bike stroking their way across the county.

Samuelson and Arshen, keenly interested in maintaining the status of *Editors for Hire*, hired consultants who amassed data showing how to keep their firm highly respected. It needed to be well-managed, and for that, they hired Sonia Glick, herself an author with three fairly well-received novels to brag about. She knew her craft, worked hard, and had a reputation among writers for having a magical touch in pairing writers and editors. Sonia could wine and dine agents and publishers when she needed to, but the editors who worked for her preferred to keep limited contact with Sonia. She could be volatile, a Genghis Khan about deadlines. She was often testy or rageful, lacerating an editor for a missed comma, yet other times her praise was risible, once notoriously calling an editor the Michelangelo of paragraphing.

The other editors observed Sonia's behavior but didn't have the label Helen had. Years before at an annual holiday party Sonia, tipsy mid-way through the party, lured Helen into a one-on-one conversation and told her about her bi-polar diagnosis. Helen had guessed it, but once she knew, she secretly studied Sonia. Would she be able to tell when Sonia took her medication? She learned to read Sonia's necklaces and knew when Sonia was off her meds and in a manic mode, she'd wear three or four brightly colored necklaces with coin charms, but when she was depressed, it would be a single dark wooden necklace. This necklace wearing happened about twice a year. The rest of the time Sonia seemed to take her meds. Part of Helen's motive in studying Sonia was to gain information she might use later in monitoring Kristen's medications.

Helen was in awe that Sonia functioned as well as she did. She was the only editor genuinely fond of Sonia who thought Sonia was nearly brilliant, the way a pyramid that momentarily catches light on all sides is brilliant.

They were both keenly aware that each had something on the other. Helen knew Sonia's diagnosis, and because Sonia had inappropriately answered Helen's cell one day, Sonia knew something was amiss about Helen's daughter, but she knew nothing more than that.

When Helen got to *Sonata*, she saw Sonia near the door to the restaurant.

"Helen! Helen, over here," Sonia called out.

"Jeans?" Helen called over to Sonia as she locked her car and walked toward the door of *Sonata*.

"I've never seen you in jeans before," Helen added once she'd joined Sonia at the door of the restaurant.

"I found this online store," Sonia said, her voice uncharacteristically chirpy.

There were no necklaces. Helen was confused by Sonia's frantic voice and gestures, yet her neck was bare. She looked closely at Sonia's eyes, which were dilated and seemed animated by emotions Helen couldn't define.

"Not now," Helen said under her breath.

"Yes, it had to be now," Sonia echoed without catching Helen's meaning as they went into the restaurant and got their table.

After they'd talked a while, Helen asked about her next assignment.

"That's why I wanted to meet, Helen. I'm going to need more time assigning you now. What I had in mind for you just didn't fit you the more I thought about it. I only came to see this about an hour ago, and I figured you'd be on the road already, so I decided I'd treat you to a nice farm-fresh dinner, and we'll meet again as soon as a good match comes up for you."

Helen wasn't pleased by making this long trip for nothing, but she wasn't the boss.

Sonia, who had gone off in her own world, chatted away while their dinner was served. Helen watched Sonia, all animated with her lips smacking and her hands pointing, jabbing, or circling to make some point. All the while she was thinking that though Sonia knew something wasn't right about her daughter, what she did not know is that Helen knew Sonia's boss, Dick Arshen, very well.

Helen and Dick had grown up in the same small town and gone all through school together. Dick was the boy who wanted so badly to be elected president of their class. Helen was the girl who seemed to do everything effortlessly. She was usually elected vice-president of the class, and was even elected president in their sophomore year. Dick was in awe of that. He developed a hard crush on Helen that culminated in their senior year, when he was finally elected president of the class. Helen was his vice-president. She was also his girlfriend by then, and the night of the senior prom, she became his lover after an evening fueled by cocaine.

What would Sonia think if only she knew I was Dick Arshen's lover in high school?

This was the only thing on Helen's mind as Sonia babbled on.

Finally, Sonia noticed the slight smile on Helen's lips.

"What's so funny, Helen?"

"Funny?" Helen said.

Sonia began smiling, and Helen cocked her head.

"What's so funny to you?" Helen asked.

"Funny?" Sonia answered, thinking if only Helen knew I have a mad crush on my new hire, Penny.

Chapter Six

When Helen reached home after her meeting with Sonia, it was after 10 p.m. It had been a long day, and she sat on her sitting room sofa with a cup of tea before going to bed. She never made it to bed and that night Helen had a dream that Hank was spooning in bed with her.

She woke suddenly, and she tried to shake the dream off. There was a deeply gray sky outside. She heard the sound of raindrops hitting her windows at a slant, and could smell petrichor, that earthy scent when rain moistens dry land. This was the weather the morning Hank was killed.

It was a gruesome death. Hank, a building contractor, died in agony but not instantly the July before. It was the most careless of accidents. Those who witnessed it said he had looked down to his right-side seconds before. Helen knew that he was checking his schedule for the day He kept his business calendar on the passenger seat. Witnesses also said that she, in a van filled with three children, had turned her body almost fully around, facing the back of the van, presumably telling her children to stop fighting. They stopped fighting, killed instantly along with their mother. Only the baby survived, motherless now. Hank survived until the ambulance arrived. The cab of his truck had crushed his lower body, and the ambulance crew could not get him out. He screamed in agony until he was pronounced dead at 10:23 a.m. The last thing she'd said to him, just three hours earlier, was, "I've got meetings all afternoon, so for Christ's sake, please pick up some cat food before Dumpster starves."

Helen could not get past the two memories, how Hank suffered the last moments of his life and what her last words to him had been. Those memories blocked her grieving and made her sorrow bury like lead in her stomach. She hadn't found the words to understand Hank's death within herself. Helen kept everyone out of her chaotic grief by acting as if she were healing back to her old self, a self she knew had unraveled into bare frayed threads like old wires. She had asked Carmie to give the news of Hank's death to Kristen. Carmie said she had, but Helen had never asked how Kristen reacted because she could not take any more grief onboard.

She always thought she and Hank would have time to heal from the rupture of their trust over Kristen's treatment. They had healed some, but they never got anywhere near the magic they had when they first met.

Henrik (Hank) Nicolas Di Palma and Helen Stark Baird met at college at the end of their junior year. Hank had transferred in January of junior year, and Helen heard girls giggling about him, but she didn't catch sight of him until the final week of junior year as he strode across the quad. *That must be him,* she thought, when she saw him heading toward the library.

"A Greek god," girls in the dorm trilled about him to one another.

"You are all just absurd romantics," Helen would say in the third-floor lounge. "There's no such thing as romantic love. It's just a trope made up in the 12th century by the Troubadours." Helen often took herself very seriously as an English major, and she could turn the champagne-dreams of her third-floor colleagues flat in less than a minute.

However, when she saw Hank heading for the library that day, she whispered, "My God, they are right." Hank, broad-shouldered and trim at 6'4", was a man of golden good looks, and he was beautiful. Helen headed for the library where they met in the stacks while looking for biographies of F. Scott Fitzgerald, but it wasn't until the following fall, at the beginning of their senior year that they became a couple.

Neither was looking for love and certainly not for a steady partner. While Hank was still in his teens, women offered themselves to him, which startled him out of any desire he might otherwise have felt, so he remained a virgin until he was eighteen. Then he had several short-term encounters, which he ended when he found the women boring, lacking in fortitude and originality, qualities he adored in his Swedish mother. He became frustrated after he'd become aroused by the looks of a woman but in time found nothing of character, courage, humor, and kindness in her. When he met those qualities in Helen, that was the end of Hank's looking.

Helen had had her share of admirers though she might not have been considered beautiful. It depended on who appraised her. She was sometimes described as handsome rather than beautiful though there was no masculinity about her. It was something in her expression that led people to hem and haw and finally latch onto *handsome* to describe her. At 5'9", Helen was taller than most women. Her face had classic features, yet they were somewhat asymmetrical. Her hair, which was brown indoors, became reddish brown when she was in sun. She had a pleasing but far from perfect body: her hips were slightly too large and her breasts slightly too small. In stillness, one might say she was attractive, but it was when she smiled, laughed, walked, bent, and spoke in her naturally musky voice that she was called beautiful—and irresistibly to some—because it was in motion and in speaking that Helen's sensuality and character emerged.

When Helen fell in love with Hank, she was more surprised than anyone she knew. She'd vaguely planned a life around scholarship, for she fancied herself a scholar in making. Helen thought the best she could expect from her twenties was sexual experimentation with interesting partners, but she didn't believe in or expect *love.* Yet there it was, in her heart and in her mind.

Their meeting was essentially the first day of their thirty-two-year marriage though they didn't legally marry until two years later. They were passionate with one another early on.

She wondered whether the eventual dimming of their erotic joy was only a matter of her having found nothing else important once Kristen was ill. Since she'd been battling Kristen's difficulties, she had not been up to what she demanded of herself, and not able to give Hank what she'd promised him in her vows. It was that her life force had dimmed, nearly to extinction.

Was this, she thought, *how Hank felt, too*, or had he always been more reserved, restrained than Helen? For someone with the body of a Greek god, Hank had been peculiarly modest. He often came to her with his T-shirt tucked soundly into his cotton pajamas, which made her understand that his mother had had a protocol leading to bedtime. Even when Hank didn't shower in the evening, it always seemed as if he'd just toweled himself off with a 100% Turkish cotton towel and traced his mother's gestures of smoothing and then soundly tucking his T-shirt beneath the waist of his pajama bottoms, so when he pulled back the covers to their bed, Helen saw him as a boy-man climbing in bed with her. In their early years, Helen could banish the boy with a simple turning of her hips toward Hank, whose face changed as if he had never really met himself before, as his arousal made him move her solidly against him.

In love-making Hank abandoned every inch of every part of himself to her. She relished the jagged thrusts his hips made to enter her ever more deeply and the bellows of his lungs when he came, but especially the high-pitched groans and shaking twists of his body right after coming, as if he were a vessel tossing to right itself in waters that nearly wrestled it to the ocean floor.

From the time of his yelps of the last of coming and his fierce clinging to her, nearly an hour passed before he returned her body to her, or seemed remotely like himself again, so far into woods of longing had he been transported. But when he searched for his T-shirt and pajama bottoms, Helen, without stirring a muscle or looking for a shred of her own prior clothing, smiled at the return of the boy in the man. But for his caring, careful, soothing and scrupulous mother, Helen might have had the lover of her dreams.

Later, when their wars over Kristen's treatment came, they seemed to lose everything that had been between them. Hank called out the loss of his trust in Helen. Helen became distant, taking with her the warmth she'd always opened to him. When their impasse over Kristen ended with her diagnosis, they had different views of how to go forward from the diagnosis. Helen buried herself inside the folds of her inner life. Hank felt that now they knew, they had no choice but to go on with as much energy as they could muster in their future.

Silent times and fights broke out again.

For a long time, Helen remained morose. Hank tried to cheer her or at least talk her into pretending to get up and live on.

Helen found this mentality irksome to the point that she wanted to tell him to shut up.

All he could do at first was try to see bright spots. "But, Helen, maybe they'll be able to help her in some way." "Helen, there's nothing more we can do now." "Helen, you cannot let this destroy you. That won't help Kristen." "Helen, where are you? Please try to talk to me." "Helen, take this. The doctor prescribed it for you. It might help you." "Helen. Helen. Helen."

She learned from this that it isn't true people suffering the same grief can help each other.

She just wanted to be alone. She wanted Hank to go away.

Then he died.

After Hank's death, Helen let all passion die in her until she had to feel it again because she had to find Kristen.

Chapter Seven

The rain stopped, and Helen thought she would spend some time in her garden after the sun dried things out. She was in her closet looking for some gardening clothes when the cell she'd left it on her bed rang.

"Let them leave a message," she was about to say, but something made her trot back to the bed to answer it.

"You're an idiot," the well-known voice on the other end said.

"I know, Carmie. I know."

"I'm not going to ask what made you go in on your own. I'm not going to tell you that you put back our chances of actually talking with Kristen by years. I'm not going to tell you how much harder you've made my work, but I am going to request that you not meet with new mothers until after they've been in the support group for at least six months because obviously, Helen, you don't know what to tell them."

"Do you really think I've put us back years?"

"Yes. I'm going in today myself to try to see if I can get any info on Kristen's reaction of having her mother chase her down Broadway for all the world to see, right before a cop scored a take-down on that mother."

"Oh, Jeez."

"So, Helen, I'm not much for that mumbo-jumbo therapy you're so high on, but since you're doing it, why not ask your shrink if you secretly want to change places with me. I mean, start seeing in-take mothers and going into the City to do tracking because if so, come take my room here in the convent, and I'll move into your house."

"Oh, of course not, Carmie."

"Well, then, figure out something to do with your life because you sure are stepping on my toes now."

"Yes, I see that, and I'm sorry. Would you really give up your mission?"

"Not the mission, but I'm sure toying with giving up living in this convent with these weirdos. Anyway, got to run if I'm to get a full day in."

"Call me later?"

"Yup."

Helen frowned and clicked off the phone.

***

Carmie got into her orange and cream VW bus and headed into the City.

A few years before, a woman in Carmie's support group raised her hand in a session and said she had a question.

"Sister, may I make a guess about where you get information in the City?"

"Go ahead," Carmie said, "but I'll never tell anyone my sources."

"Soup kitchens!" The woman was thrilled with herself and looked around the room for the approval of the other mothers.

Carmie stood there stunned, trying to keep a straight face, all the while thinking, hey, there's an idea.

Since then she always hit the upper West side soup kitchens.

Parking six blocks from Joe's 90th and Broadway kitchen, Carmie wondered whether she'd get anything out of Old Joe today. Joe, the top of his head gleaming and bald, two white slicks of long white hair running over his ears to the back of his head, was stocking the shelves this morning at the soup kitchen on Broadway and 90th.

"Hey, Joe."

"Oh, yeah, hi ya, Sista. What's doin'?"

"Just trying to find out how much damage one of my mothers did last week."

"Haven't seen Kristen in here, but the other kids talking a lot. Pretty bad, Sista. I think it was pretty bad."

"Who's been in talking, Joe?"

"Lots of them."

"Guys? Gals? Myra's group? Naomi's group?"

"Some from all them groups, Sista."

"Edifying, Joe."

"Nope, no Eddie come by."

"Well look, Joe, if you can't be specific about what they said," Carmie was looking up at the ceiling when Joe wheeled around, taking offense at what she said, "can you tell me something, exactly something one of them said?"

Carmie lowered her head and saw Joe's angry face.

"That's it, Sista," he said. "All I can tell you; it was bad."

"Had to be. Well, if you hear anything more specific, would you call me?"

"Yeah, okay, sista."

Carmie left the soup kitchen mumbling, "Yeah okay, sista, sure thing." She knew Joe never spilled what he heard. He'd do just what he did then, let on that he'd heard things in general, but never give info that jangled wires. She got a half block from the soup kitchen, turned around, and made an uncivil gesture at it.

She knew she should get to the soup kitchen further uptown, but there, too, she never got info that gave her anything more than *everyone said something*.

"Nah," she muttered. "Going directly to Duane Reade."

It was at Duane Reade, the drug store further downtown, where Carmie usually struck it rich.

It was Minnie, a clerk at the pharmacy, who knew everything going on.

"Girls got to get their birth-control pills, right?" Minnie always said.

Minnie had a way with her, and Carmie could never figure out how Minnie ticked.

Carmie hiked down to Duane Reade, pushed the double glass door open, walked to the back of the store where the pharmacy was and got in the pharmacy line. There were three in front of her, but they had no connection to the street kids, Carmie knew. It would be a wait, so she went back up front, grabbed a PEOPLE magazine, told the check-out guy she'd pay at the pharmacy and headed back to the line. Now there were four in front of her, but that would give her time to catch up on gossip.

So, this Meghan girl all over the map. "Put down roots somewhere," Carmie counselled.

Then there was the long-standing case of that little abducted girl and getting closer to fingering the monster who took her.

"Rot in hell is my advice to you, buster," Carmie said under her breath.

"Oh, Sister," the woman behind her tapped her on the shoulder. "Forgiveness above all, isn't it, Sister?"

Carmie turned fully around and then some to get the woman in the vision of her one eye.

"There are exceptions, ma'am," was all Carmie said.

"Really?" the lady said. "I never knew there could be exceptions. Well, then, my brother-in-law, George, can rot in hell right along with your fella."

Carmie nodded her head, "and may they keep each other company as their toes burn off. HA!"

"Yes, HA," the lady said.

Carmie often thought it was a good thing she couldn't tell anyone her methods of sleuthing because no one would guess standing at the Duane Reade pharmacy refining theoretical beliefs of people in line would be one of her methods.

Carmie had time to read that the Queen was okay. Though Carmie's heritage was Italian she liked the Queen a lot more than the current Pope. Just before the person ahead of her finished up, Carmie turned to surveil those behind her in line. Nothing but old men and women. She quickly put her PEOPLE on a nearby shelf so she'd look businesslike.

"Ah, Sister Carmie." Minnie smiled as Carmie pressed against the counter. Minnie was no taller than 5'2" and as skinny as a broom handle. She dyed her hair red, a red that screeched "bottle," and her skin was so crisscrossed with wrinkles that she looked like a map.

"So, Minnie, I'm here today about,"

"Kristen, I know. I know all about the mother. Whoa. Mistake there."

"Yeah, so I'm here to find out how bad."

"Bad, Sister. Real bad. So bad Kristen hasn't been in to pick up her birth control pills. She gets a six-month supply, so she was due for the next six-months three days ago."

"Oh, dear. So how much damage do you think?"

"I'll know something tomorrow. If she doesn't pick up her six-month prescription tomorrow, I'll have to send it back, and then we'll have something to talk about. All the kids were talking about it. They're all hiding out more deeply for a while. I mean, Kristen's mother may be clumsy as hell, but she ain't a murderer, and they know that. Some of these kids have to worry that way, ya know?"

"Yeah, I know. Look, Minnie, you know I usually keep a lid on this kind of thing. Helen got away from me, but I'll double-down on her and the others about coming in."

"You know what, Sister Carmie, if I may say so. Bring her in with you from time to time. This will make her less anxious, and she'll feel she's doing something. You know what I mean?"

"Hmm. Never looked at it that way, Minnie. I'll give it a think. And look. Would you be able to give me a call tomorrow with whatever you pick up?"

"Oh, I will, Sister. I'll get as much as I can on Kristen, and I'll call."

Carmie grabbed her PEOPLE magazine and forgetting to pay for it at Minnie's register, took it up front.

"Okay. What'll it be?" she asked the checker up front.

"Just put it back, Sister," the man at the register said. "We all like a little gossip, yes?"

"Oh, yeah. Hey, how much does a pack of bubble gum cost?"

Pleased with her potential catch of the day, Carmie decided to move home slowly. Maybe when she got off the highway in the country, she'd treat herself to a drive around. Truth was, she hated being in the convent. As time went by, she wondered more and more about her vows. It was what kids these days called a "rebound." For Carmie, entering the convent was a rebound from her violent early sexual encounters. She'd wanted to be safe from men, from sex, from her own wild impulses. She figured this life as a nun would preserve her as she was when she first went home to her mother—wiser, not panting like a pig for sex, but having a life that was worth something, a life to be proud of.

After she got off the highway with these thoughts tumbling around, she turned left, not right, at the fork. She wanted to ramble. She wanted to roam.

"Damn it," she said to her rearview mirror. "I do not want to go to that convent."

A car swerved in front of her, and she slammed on the brakes.

"Watch the light, dimwit," a man yelled at her. She'd almost driven through a red light.

"You watch your lights, buster," she screamed back at him, "or I'll put them out for you!"

She was unhappy, very unhappy. "I want a different life," she whispered as she headed back to the convent.

Chapter Eight

Helen never got into her garden after she'd been scolded by Carmie because Sheila, Kristen's old friend from 6th grade, called. Sheila was a teacher at the local high school and lived in town near her mother. She told Helen that Paula, a high-powered lawyer in Washington, D.C., was in town for a day or two, and they'd like to come by to see Helen. The girls from Kristen's idyllic 6th grade occasionally came by to see Helen, but it had been years since she'd seen Paula.

They arranged that the girls, well, Helen corrected her thinking because they were fully young women now, would come by and have lunch with her. Sheila insisted she would bring sandwiches from the local deli. Helen asked for a BLT on rye. She'd go down into Hank's old wine cellar and bring up a nice Chardonnay to go with lunch.

Helen showered and put on a new sundress, a cotton in a very deep teal. Her stomach felt fluttery at the prospect of seeing "the girls." Since she was in jail, she'd been examining herself more closely and was finding traits she didn't like. But she was very happy when she looked deep within, she found nothing but good wishes for the girls in Kristen's old group. She examined this hard because she thought it would be natural for her to feel jealousy about their successful lives, maybe even, on a bad day, feel pleasure to hear that something had gone wrong for them, but she found none of this. She only found genuine fondness, happiness and good wishes for them all.

When Helen saw the girls pull up in Sheila's car, she swung open her front door before the girls had rung the bell. Stepping forward, she opened her arms wide and embraced both young women at once.

"Oh, so good to see my girls," she bellowed with laughter.

"Mom Helen," Sheila said, returning her hug. "So good to see you as always." Sheila, a dirty blonde whose skin almost matched her hair tone, was spindly thin and came across at first as meek. Helen knew she was strong in many ways. She had what seemed like a good marriage and one young son. She also had a successful teaching career, and Helen thought she remembered that Sheila had been made Chair of her area. Still, most people underrated Sheila as someone who didn't matter that much.

Paula, on the other hand, reeked self-esteem, self-will, and know-how. She was a sturdy woman, not fat in any way, but large-boned, and she stood as if she had a lance hidden behind her back. She had bobbed auburn hair, piercing green eyes, which she held in a steady gaze, and she carried herself as if she were just about to challenge you to a 500-foot sprint that she was bound to win.

"Oh, girls," Helen backed out of the embrace to look each in the eye. "So good to see you. Come on in, and let me get us all some wine." Helen led them to the kitchen, took a chilled Chardonnay from the fridge and picked up a tray with three glasses and a wine bottle opener.

"Come, follow me. We'll be comfortable in the sitting room," and she led them up the three stairs to the wide room with its expansive views.

"Oh, I always loved this room," Paula said, looking out on the meadow. "Kristen was so lucky," she said.

Lucky? Helen stubbed her toe on a foot of the coffee table before she gained her balance.

"You okay?" Sheila asked.

"Just clumsy." Helen laughed. "Now sit down and tell me everything that's going on."

Both sat on the couch, and Helen pulled up the rocker to be near them.

"How is Kristen?" Sheila asked. Paula chimed in, "Yes, how is Kristen doing?"

Helen wished they could just avoid this question and keep their gathering a superficial show and tell.

"Well, I don't really know. We're not in communication," Helen said with as much equanimity as she could.

Sheila and Paula lowered their heads at the same time, which made Helen want to shout through the room, 'She's not dead. She's just lost.'

"So, Paula," Helen said, "What's it like to be a big important lawyer for those politicians?"

"Oh, my main client is the State Department," Paula said matter-of-factly. "State Department personnel."

54

"So interesting," Helen said, noting that Sheila looked away from the conversation, got up and went to the window to look over the meadow.

Helen decided to ignore her for the moment and concentrate on Paula.

"What kind of cases do you do?"

Paula talked for a full ten minutes about her recent cases, how important they were, how all men in Washington were jerks, how she had no one to date, how long her hours were, and how when you got right down to it, how boring her work was.

Helen was listening intently for something Paula said she could latch onto and bring to a positive point, but at the end of Paula's diatribe, all she could say was, "I see." She decided to switch gears, "And how is your wonderful mother?"

"Oh, God," Paula said. "She is just full of complaints."

Helen's eyebrows shot up.

"Her hips hurt. So, I say, well, have them done. She says, I'm scared to have them replaced. Then she says, it wouldn't help. I've got arthritis everywhere. So, I say, well, do yoga. Oh, it's too expensive. It's a real drag to be around her."

"Oh!" Helen said. She recalled how proud Sandra always was and thought how shamed she'd feel to hear her daughter talk about her this way.

Helen swung her body around to address Sheila.

"And how about you, Sheila? What's going on?"

Sheila came over and sat down on the couch. She looked as if she might cry.

"What's wrong dear?" Helen asked.

"I still can't get pregnant," she said.

"But you have your wonderful Gregory," Helen said.

"I know. I know," Sheila said plaintively. "But really, who wants an only child?"

Helen's shoulders tightened. *No one*, she thought, *but some of us can't have more than one.*

She kept her mouth in a firm smile. It was really Hank who couldn't have another child. His sperm count was too low.

"I just don't think one child equals a family," Sheila said.

Helen saw that Sheila was so self-absorbed by her disappointment that she had no idea how her words were affecting Helen. Even Paula, who always looked as if she'd just had a hearty luncheon of trout and endive salad, had turned slightly red and looked askance at Sheila.

"Well, I'm just miserable about it," Sheila went on.

"I'm the unluckiest woman on earth, and Robert drives me crazy with always trying to get me to see the bright side. There is no bright side," she finished and began to weep. "Pardon me. Is there a tissue?"

Helen pointed to the desk against the front wall with its box of tissues.

She was afraid what she was thinking might leak out all over the room, or she might scream, *Kristen may be the unluckiest woman on earth, but you aren't.*

Both girls were glumly silent when Sheila came back with the box of tissues and sat on the couch next to Paula.

Helen's stomach was so riled up she thought she couldn't eat, but she was eager to move this gathering along so she could be alone again.

"Shall we eat lunch?" she said brightly.

Paula waited for Sheila to get up to get the sandwiches from her car, but she just sat there sobbing.

"Okay, I'll get the sandwiches," Paula said. "Give me the keys, Sheila."

"Oh, I'll get them," Sheila said, getting up. "Count on me to run and fetch," she said, leaving the room with an almost visible gray plume trailing her.

Chapter Nine

Helen closed the door as Sheila and Paula left, calling back, "Bye Mom Helen. We'll be in touch." These girls, all five of the 6th grade girls, were more important to Helen than almost anyone she knew. In a vault in Helen's mind, there was a timeline. It began in vibrant colors at Kristen's birth but turned gray and dull at the end of the summer after 6th grade. When Helen thought of the 6th grade girls, she could stay in the brightly colored part of her timeline and keep Kristen there, too, before the world turned gray. Helen counted on these girls to keep the color in her mind. Seeing how self-absorbed and unhappy they were today terrified Helen because if they couldn't keep their own lives vibrant to themselves, how could they possibly keep the memory of Kristen vibrant? They were each, in their own minds, the unluckiest girl in the world, and neither had even a thought for Kristen, not really, or they couldn't have said some of the things that they said. Were they even Kristen's friends, or were they ever Kristen's friends?

These 6th grade girls had access to Helen that others did not have. After Helen and Hank learned what Kristen's diagnosis was, they didn't speak to anyone about it because they couldn't bear the reactions. People who prodded Helen to name Kristen's disease would then say, "A what? How can that be?" But it was. It just was.

When Kristen started running away, Helen invited all of the 6th grade girls in Kristen's group over to the house. She wanted these girls to understand what happened to Kristen because she wanted them to be kind to her. She told them what she thought happened, that Kristen's illness most likely began that idyllic summer after graduation from Brook Mount, which she, her own mother, had orchestrated. Helen pieced together the likely scenario. Kristen ran carefree and seemingly forever young through the meadows and woods, trailing her green kite behind her. Then, at some point, she flopped down on their long rye grass, out of breath, but still laughing. It was the same exact spot that one of the deer who nestled on their land each night had lain the night before. The deer was infested with ticks, and a tick, perhaps just one, fell off the body of the deer and nestled into the grass, that very grass on her meadow that Kristen, in her sublime abandon, lay on, holding her belly filled with hilarious laughter about something her friends said. She rolled over, and the legs of the shorts bunched up around her legs, exposing her upper thigh, bare and plump, and the tick, looking for blood, bit her.

The next night, Kristen said she felt itching on her leg. Helen had asked, "Where?" Kristen had hemmed and hawed and said, "Well, up there, near up there." Helen's eyes raced to the edge of Kristen's short shorts and saw only Kristen's smooth skin, and it struck Helen suddenly that Kristen was becoming slowly nubile during this summer. Because of where Kristen said her itching was, Helen forced herself into a new mother persona, the one that she was just then practicing, the mother persona of backing off and letting go, and she remembered how proud she was of her choice to treat Kristen as a developing young woman and not a little girl. She didn't say what was on her tongue, "Well, show me. I need to see the place that's itching." Instead, she turned her head away from Kristen in nonchalance, and said over her shoulder, "Well, I'm sure you can take care of it."

Helen had been so proud of her affect that evening when she all but said, see, Kristen, I'm respecting your growing maturity. But Kristen wasn't an adult. She was still a little girl. She was a little girl who needed her mother to say Well show me. I need to see the place that's itching. When Helen told Paula, Nicky, Jen, and Sheila this part of the story, they all looked wide-eyed as if they were thinking, why didn't you check where it was itching. My mother would have. Helen remembered that moment of their wide-eyed stares at her as the moment that catapulted Helen into her own battle for sanity. Helen knew Kristen's illness was her fault. She blamed herself for every part of Kristen's tragedy. The sharp internal words she hurled at herself—*stupid, pig-headed, dense, naïve, gullible*—would have made anyone sick, and they made Helen very sick for years after Kristen had become a permanent runaway.

At one point, her guilt outweighed everything else in her, and she could no longer stand it. She was driving on a highway on her way home from a work meeting, watching an oncoming truck. The hulking metallic mouth of the truck, wending its way down the highway, approached her, slowly and ponderously, glints from the sun on its hood like longitudinal lunges from the sky. The truck was hungry, and it was ready for her, just a tasty morsel, a tease for the cavernous body that trailed behind the grated mouth. Why not. So simple. Just fail to turn the wheel around a bend; her side mirror would catch on the huge side chrome bumper, a dynamic that would twirl her into a final slam, bang, dunk.

She turned her wheel at the last moment and saved herself, but for what? Helen valued her own life so little. She couldn't think of why she was living. Her marriage was in shambles and she'd made her daughter irretrievably sick. Every day was filled with emotional and increasingly more prominent physical pain. She had been so tense for so long that she thought the stiffness in her legs was only stress. She drank a half bottle to a bottle of wine every single night beginning the night she returned from Rochester, but that didn't relieve her stress, stiffness, and pain. It just made her dreary.

She was dragged to the doctor by Hank.

When the doctor ordered an MRI, Helen had no idea what they were looking for. She remembered the test though. Her mind in a fog, she stood outside a room wearing a gown that slit up the back. Someone was holding her arm, and an animal panic of exposure had made her hands flit to each side of the slit to cover her bareness as she was taken into a room which was dark and silent—like a concert hall the moment before the conductor takes the podium.

"You getting pains again?" this person holding her arm asked.

"Who are you?" Helen recalled asking, which made whoever roll her eyes.

"I'm the person helping you on the table," she said. "Now come on."

Helen knew that whatever was happening was inevitable, so she made her breathing as silent as it could be and stretched her legs out on the table that suddenly ushered her into a cold dark chamber. Then the first tick stunningly broke silence, and another; another until the tick became drawn into an ambient undertone. A beat was on. A louder, deeper, almost moaning electrical sound faded to a reverberation while new, clean, nervous notes rolled into a flange. The loud sound looped into a sequence, moaning, fading, reverberating while the new clean nervous sound twisted and trilled on the flange, filling the sonic groove with its tension. Helen's ears were virgin to this world where sounds deployed into stars, the ones you can see right away and then the ones you can't see until after some minutes, and the ones that had never been there. Too abruptly, everything stopped. She was moving in jerks back out of this place. The lights outside burned her eyes.

A week later, Helen was sitting in a chair in her doctor's office. Hank tried to explain to her what the doctor might tell them, but she didn't understand him. From the time she heard the word, *borrelia*, it was as if everyone around her spoke in tongues, including Hank. The doctor came in, stood behind his desk, and said, "We have some good news."

"There is no good news," Helen said. "We've got *borrelia*!"

"Well the good news," the doctor continued, "is that you do not have multiple sclerosis."

"Okay, but doctor, even though I'm fine, I am not fine! I've still got *borrelia*," Helen said.

"Well not so quick, Helen," her doctor said softly. "You do not have *borrelia*. Your daughter does. You also do not have lesions in your spine, or any other evident disease that would cause the pain and stiffness you've been experiencing, but I think this means you have fibromyalgia, and it has been going on for some time now."

"So?" Helen said. The fibro-whatever didn't matter at all to Helen. She had no interest in dealing with it. The doctor prescribed something called Lyrica, and she agreed to take it only because she was too tired to argue about it, but as for learning what fibromyalgia was like, so that she could understand her condition, she couldn't fathom that.

She was at war with *borrelia* and would remain in battle with it.

When she told her doctor this, he said he hoped in that case that her pain wouldn't be too debilitating.

But it was and continued to be debilitating.

Some mornings Helen had to roll from her bed and put one leg on the floor before she could inch herself into a standing position. Pain became normal and came in as many flavors as ice cream in summer. One flavor of pain that made her buckle every time it came was the electrical pain that came suddenly like a kick in the gut. She'd had thunderbolts hit the center of her eyeball and frizzes of electric shocks up and down her spine. She'd been hit in the groin with jolts that seemed to ricochet to her knees and then dart to the balls of her feet. It was as if her entire body were experiencing a severe thunder storm.

This was the cost of her guilt. Helen hadn't told Paula, Jen, Nikki, and Sheila that she was responsible for Kristen's disease, but they knew. When they looked at her, she knew they were thinking, our mothers would have checked where our leg itched. We would never have gotten *borrelia burgdorfi* psychosis because our mothers would have turned up the edges of our shorts and looked at that upper leg under a bright light. We would have been taken to old Doc. Jenkins to get antibiotics, and we would have been saved by our mothers.

After this day's visit from Sheila and Paula, Helen was not sure whether she cared about these young women she'd had lunch with or if it was only the 6th grade girls in her mind that she cared about.

Chapter Ten

The old grandfather clock in the formal living room struck 4 p.m. and Helen's relapse into her volatile past triggered by her morning with Sheila and Paula, was broken by the house phone ringing.

"Sonia! I was wondering when you'd set up our meeting over my next job."

"Yes, Helen, we'll set up that meeting, and I'm calling about that, but there's something else."

"Oh?"

"Look, Helen, I know I shouldn't be mixing business and something personal."

Helen waited for Sonia to continue, but when she didn't, Helen said:

"It's fine, Sonia. We've known each other for how long now? And we've had some, I guess you'd say personal conversations mixed in with business. And that hasn't changed our business relationship, right?"

"I sure hope that's true, Helen. Well, I just see I really don't have friends anymore. I used to, but I work all the time. Never had time for friends, you know what I mean?"

"Yes, of course, Sonia."

"And I know I've shared my condition with you. Shouldn't have!! But I know at one of the holiday parties I had a little too much to drink, and spilled my guts to you."

On the other end of the phone, Helen's thought, *a LITTLE too much to drink?* made her eyes and mouth pop wide, but she said:

"Oh, these things always happen at holiday parties, Sonia. It's a meme!"

A few days before, Sonia had tried to explain to Helen what a meme was, so she and Helen both laughed at Helen's use of the term.

"Well, meme or not, Helen, I appreciate your being partly my friend through our long professional relationship."

"So, what's on your mind, Sonia?"

"It's a bit of a long story."

"Well, I've got nothing else going, Sonia, so shoot."

"I know I told you, drunkenly anyway, that I'm bi-polar."

"Yup."

"I don't know why, but every once in a while, I just won't take my meds."

"I know."

"What do you mean, you know? Do I show it that much?"

"It does show sometimes, Sonia, though I'm sure the others don't recognize it the way I do."

"Because of your daughter?"

"Well, hold on now, Sonia. My daughter's issue is different, and,"

"Yeah, I know, you won't talk about her."

"That's right."

"Okay, so anyway. Where was I? Oh, yes. Did you meet the newest editor I hired? Penny Lambert? Really pretty girl, uh, young woman, about 28, very blonde, medium height, really great figure."

Helen was smiling at the other end. "Does she have any editing skills as well, Sonia?"

Sonia laughed. "Oh, yes. Harvard. Then M.A. from Columbia. Lit of course. Writer herself."

"Well, anyway, to answer your question, no I haven't met her."

"I hired her back in February."

"Don't know her."

"Well, she is a friendly girl, woman really, and a few months ago, she started offering a little advice about how I dress."

"That was a little presumptuous, wasn't it?"

"Yeah, but I was in manic, hadn't done the meds, and I was lapping it up."

"Oh."

"Yeah, oh."

Helen asked, "The jeans?" referring to Sonia's very uncharacteristic outfit when they last met to discuss a project.

"Yeah, well," Sonia continued, "It wasn't just the jeans. I've spent over $5000.00 on clothes in the last month and a half."

"That's a lot, Sonia."

"Don't I know it, now that I'm trying to return half of them."

"Why return them. Do you like them?"

"They don't suit me, Helen. You know how I look. I'm not such a glamorous thing. And that's not all, Helen. And this you won't believe. I'm a platinum blonde now!"

"What!" Helen couldn't help herself and laughed uproariously.

"Oh, I know. You better believe it. That's what got me back on the meds. Holy crap. Woke up this morning wearing five or six necklaces, and looked in the mirror and nearly crapped. Got an appointment next week to have it dyed back brown."

"Well now, wait a minute, Sonia. Blondes have more fun, I've heard," Helen teased Sonia.

"Yeah, well, just shut it," Sonia teased back.

The two laughed, briefly.

"Oh, Helen." Sonia sighed. "That's not all."

"Oh, God," Helen said.

"When I was off the meds, I gave Penny a job that should have come to you."

Helen was silent.

"I had to come clean to you, Helen. I like you too much, and that's why I'm really calling. To apologize to you and to tell you I'm giving you two jobs back-to-back to make up for it. I know how good you are and how fast you are, so I know you can do this. And I'm sorry, Helen. Never happen again."

Helen was about to say she understood when Sonia continued:

"Look, Helen, I know I'm nuts. I'm more than a little nuts, but I can function, and I really care about *Editors for Hire*."

"I know you do, Sonia," Helen said before Sonia interrupted her.

"But I never had a mother, or anybody, who fussed over me or taught me how to look. I don't know how to look," Sonia said. "I never told anyone this, Helen, but I was adopted late, and before that, some foster homes, until I was four."

"Oh, Sonia, I'm sorry. I had no idea," Helen said, her ears tingling with the raw mortification in Sonia's voice, but she could think of nothing else to say.

"Both parents had mental difficulties," Sonia continued. "Mother a suicide, and Dad, I don't know where he is, but he abandoned me after Mom shot herself. No relatives, so there were lonely years in there."

"I am sorry you didn't have your parents, Sonia."

"Yeah, it was rough, but all the same, I survived."

"You sure did, Sonia, and are very successful despite all this."

"I did okay," she said, "but I know what a little fool I've been in the last month." Sonia began to laugh, "but I looked so good for about a month that I just went wild. Traded it all to have someone fuss over me," Sonia said.

Helen was tearing up, and she felt her heart bursting for Sonia's sorrow, pain, and bravery.

"Look, Sonia," she said breathlessly. "I'm having a little dinner party tomorrow, no no, the next night. Yeah, that's right, on Thursday, at 7, and I want you to come."

"Oh, that's sweet, Helen. I'd love to come. Who else is coming?"

Helen's cell phone rang, and since she had no idea who else was coming to this dinner party, she had just conceived to make Sonia feel loved, she used this other call to get off the phone.

"Hey, Sonia, I'll call you back later. Got a call coming in on the cell, and I have to take it."

"Oh, okay, Helen. Thanks for talking to me, for letting me share all this."

"Right, Sonia. Call later. Gotta get this," and Helen hung up.

Chapter Eleven

It was Carmie on the cell. She had tentative information that Kristen was traveling with a boy.

"It's only hearsay, Helen."

"I get it."

"But my source was pretty sure about it."

"God, this is hard for me."

"Yeah, Helen. Who said having kids is a warm fuzzy lamb?"

"A warm fuzzy lamb, Carmie? It's a rose garden, not a warm fuzzy lamb. Never mind. So, tell me about this fellow."

"Yeah, I hear he's some sort of street musician. Guitar, I think, or was it ukulele?"

"Is he good to her? Does he have AIDS? Is he crazy?" Helen asked.

"Don't have a whole lot on him, Helen, but I've already told you the word on Kristen is that she's tough. Takes no crap, and she can be aggressive, as I've said before."

"That's all a front," Helen said.

"Well it works."

"Are they on the streets or with someone?"

"Word is he has some kind of friends in the west 70s, and they're there for now."

"Should I come in?" Helen asked.

"Hell, no!"

"I'd be doing something,"

"Yeah, screwing things up, like before. It's a miracle I got this info. Give me a few weeks, a month or two maybe, to try to get closer to them."

"You'll call with anything?"

"As always, Helen. Oh, and I hear he's black."

Helen paused. Then she said, "That means he's beautiful. Kristen always liked beautiful, and by the way, Carmie, no one plays the ukulele these days."

"Well how the hell should I know. I'm the kid who had no father and whose mother hid out in a laundry room just to avoid her."

"You know, Carm, I think that's the first time ever I've heard you do self-pity."

"Well, what the hell, I'm struggling."

"What's going on, Carm?"

"I'm just so tired of everything. Everything seems the same, the same old thing. And I can't stand these nuns I live with."

"You're a nun, Carm."

"Yeah, well I'm thinking not for long."

"You serious, Carm?"

"Oh, yes, dead serious. I mean about thinking about it. Not ready to do anything yet."

"It's that bad living there?"

"Oh, it's bad living here, but should that mean leaving my vows? I don't know. I just don't know."

Helen suddenly had an idea.

"You just need a change of scenery now. Look, I'm having a small dinner party night after tomorrow. So, come. Don't wear your nun clothes and just relax with some other folks."

"Maybe. Who'll be there?"

Helen thought quickly.

"Well, what would you say if I invited, what's his name? The hairy one."

"Fred Ungar."

"Yeah, him. I'll go to a meeting tonight and see if he's there."

"Okay," Carmie said.

"And what about Janet Masland? I think she has a husband. Probably an asshole, but don't you think you can avoid an asshole if you don't sit next to him?"

"I doubt that," Carmie said, but, yeah, those two would be fine.

"Great!" Helen said.

"What can I bring?" Carmie asked.

"Bring a salad. Bring a crazy mixed-up salad, that's what," Helen said.

"Like us." Carmie laughed.

"Like us," Helen laughed with her.

Chapter Twelve

"Did you hear that, Dumpy, your girl is going around with a guy. He'd better be so good to her or I will…" She had an image of holding a club and bringing the club down swiftly and hard on his head. Her image shifted to one of the cold clammy cells she'd so recently spent the night in. okay, she said to herself, *shift gears, shift gears*, using the phrases her therapist had given her when she needed to turn her mind in a different direction.

Helen did some deep breathing, and she made herself go to a front window and look out. She concentrated looking at the street. Then beyond the street to her neighbor's lawn. Then beyond that, to the neighbor's house. These were all techniques her therapist had taught her to alter her thought patterns.

Okay, Helen thought, *this is working.* She turned to her cat who seemed to be waiting for her to keep talking to him.

"What are we going to do, Dumpster?" she said. "Haven't had a dinner party in years and years, and now I'm filling my house up with people day after tomorrow. What'll I do? Got to get some more guests for one thing. Okay, drop in at the meeting tonight, but late, and make it a quick in and out to look for Fred Ungar and Janet Masland."

Dumpster meowed plaintively. She picked him up, and he hung there awkwardly, half out of her arms.

"You don't care about my dinner party, Dumpy, do you? You care about your dinner party, right? It's time for dinner, right, Dumpy?"

Helen fed the cat. Then she sat at her island writing her menu. She'd go out shopping early the next day and cook all day. First, she'd call her cleaning service. They'd fit her in because she was one of their oldest clients.

She paused making plans for a moment and smiled. She'd been able to turn her thoughts away from worry about Kristen and into the present, into planning this party. This was a big change, and she was excited about seeing Dr. Levin this week and telling her that her techniques worked for the first time.

In the early evening, Helen got in her car and drove down the street to the Parents of Runaways evening support meeting, which was breaking up in a few minutes. When she walked into the meeting room a little after 8 p.m., Carmie was sitting behind the front table, looking stressed and lonely. Normally, she was surrounded by people with questions, but tonight no one was near her. Instead they had formed small groups talking together.

Helen spotted Fred Unger in one group and Janet Masland in another, and bee-lined for Fred first. He always reminded Helen of a big hairball. Long dark hairs covered Fred's arms, popped out of his shirt where he kept the top button undone, and masked his face to where the shape of his nose and mouth could not be discerned. Fred was a single father, and he claimed he never ate well, so when Helen invited him to her dinner party, he said he'd be happy to come. Janet was more difficult. She had a husband. Helen said to bring him. Janet said he wouldn't like it, all that talk about missing children. But after a few tense moments of Janet deliberating about whether she should come, she said, "Okay, I'll come."

When Helen got home, she called two of her editor colleagues she knew were single, Jared Klein and Tom Jiang, and both were happy to come to her party. That way she'd have three women, four counting herself, and three men.

She kept marveling at how much she'd changed—look at this, she was having a party.

Arranging this party was a huge step, and it meant she was getting better. Her therapy was paying off, and she wanted to celebrate that in her private way. She would spoil herself by changing her sheets and going to bed early, and think about how she was getting better. After a long hot shower, she got in bed, leaned against her backrest and propped herself up with several pillows, hoping to solidify her feeling of well-being.

Yes, she was slowly, slowly getting better. She'd known she needed therapy after she fantasized her truck suicide. The first therapist had been a man and though he was good, she didn't believe he could understand her feelings as a mother. She wanted a mother as her therapist, and she found a soft-spoken, highly informed, slow to speak, quick to listen woman, Dr. Frances Levin, with whom she'd been working now for about five years. Dr. Levin had three children, and the second was borderline, she shared with Helen. Although this daughter didn't run away, it was as if she had because of how she rejected her mother.

"We're up against disease," Dr. Levin often told Helen. "You have to focus on your own life," she'd tell Helen repeatedly until it had begun to sink in. "You know Kubler-Ross's five stages of grief. Well, we're making our way through them," Dr. Levin mentioned about every six months.

Helen plumped up her pillow and thought about that.

Denial was the first.

Helen just checked that off because if she thought about what her denial had cost Kristen, she would surely sink.

Anger was next. One afternoon she'd gone out into the meadow to walk off some anger, but it didn't work. She tripped over a small rock, almost fell, and picked up the rock. She threw it as hard as she could across the meadow. It skidded past a yearling, and the yearling jumped and walked closer to her mother. Helen stared at them for a long time, and seemed to see double, the deer in front of her, and the deer in the meadow the day, whatever day it was, that Kristen and her friends scampered all over this meadow. Maybe it was the mother or grandmother of this deer that had given Kristen the tick that gave her *borrelia burgdorfi* which festered in her body for years and changed the very nature of who she was.

Helen felt a rage building in her. She rushed off to the shed at the western edge of their property. Hank kept rifles locked up in a cabinet there, and she was carrying the key because she was going to do some mowing. She felt the John Deere key, on the same ring as the cabinet key, through her pant pocket, just to reassure herself they were there as she jogged. She would slaughter those deer, all of them. First the mother because the yearling would be stunned and not know where to run. She'd gun them down, one by one. "Bye-bye, Bambi!" she screamed.

At the shed, she kicked at the door, and it flew open. She marched to the rifle-cabinet, and her hands shaking, she got the key into the lock. She turned it too quickly and jammed the lock but then fiddled the key back and forth roughly and got the cabinet open. She got out Hank's favorite rifle, filled it from a nearby box of bullets, and stomped out of the shed.

They were gone. They were, all, gone.

She slammed the rifle to the ground, and it let off a shot that tore into the woods. If it had landed a few inches further to the left, it would have shot her in the leg.

Bargaining was next.

One day, she glanced out her kitchen sink window as she filled the teapot. There under a black walnut tree was a sick fawn, one she knew wouldn't last. She went to the pantry for bird seed. The oils in the seeds were nutritious for deer.

The house phone rang in the sitting room. Helen left the full teapot in the sink and ran up the stairs to answer the phone, thinking I'll be right back and save you. Then I'll make up for wanting to kill you and then Kristen will get well because I made you well.

It was someone who wanted to know if she'd planned for Medicare. No, she hadn't. Please call back. But it is imperative to plan early for these reasons. I'll research all that later. I have information now, and I can send you material to read. Just give me your address. That was Tuttle Lane or Tuttle Road? And the zip was…sorry could you repeat that? After she finally hung up, she ran back to the kitchen and looked out the window. The fawn's head had slumped further downhill. She tore out her kitchen door and ran to the slope where they fawn lay, but it had died in the time Helen was on the phone.

Getting sleepy now, Helen tried to remember what stage in Kubler-Ross came next.

"Oh, yeah," she yawned, "depression." She suddenly felt exhausted. She always felt that she was skating on a frozen pond and never knew when the moment would come when she fell through the ice into deep water.

"Depression, depression," she said, and in a few minutes was asleep.

Acceptance was next, still a long way off.

Chapter Thirteen

When Helen stirred from sleep, she imagined French toast was browning in a frying pan and would soon be streaming with real Maple syrup dripping over the edges. She remembered she was having a party, and that made her happy. She remembered she'd soon be going into Manhattan with Carmie to look for Kristen and her boyfriend.

She'd been taking long walks around her property, and the last week she went further off her property and onto a wide trail through a nearby park. She walked slowly and re-lived walks she had with her father. She could almost hear him say Look up at the birds! Look at the underside of those leaves, Helen. Go on, get off the trail and step into the woods. Go touch that lichen on the tree. Look at its color. Now squat down and watch where that line of ants goes. Follow them to see their purpose. Pick up some rocks and see them as the embodiment of all that has been.

As she was getting ready for this morning's walk, it occurred to her that at this stage of her life, these walks may be the greatest pleasure that life had to offer. She tied the laces of her new walking sneakers.

"That's okay," she said. "It's all okay."

It was about 9 a.m. when she headed out, and the light was at a slant. She could see the park ahead and was eager to get there. The area around her house was well-known for its abundance of views and trails, which brought more than a normal traffic of motorists on random days. She struck a steady pace and kept on toward the park.

She thought about her up-coming jaunt into Manhattan with Carmie and getting a glimpse of Kristen's boyfriend. She was worried that Kristen was in a harmful relationship, but if she could see for herself how this young man treated Kristen, at the slightest evidence of mis-treatment, she'd have him arrested. She tried to derail such thinking by looking at a tree in front of her, then at the bench behind that tree, then at another tree behind the bench.

Her thoughts turned to the recipes she'd chosen for her party and whether she'd be able to get the ingredients she needed.

Suddenly an approaching car on the far side of the road pulled off to the side of the road.

She squinted to see the other side of the road, and, practically blinded by the slanted morning sun, she yelled over, "You need help?"

"I wondered if it was you, Helen."

She turned her head to the side to get out of the early morning glare, but the sun remained directly in her eyes.

As a cloud blocked the sun, she saw the form of a man, a tall man with broad shoulders and a nice torso. He was looking side to side for cars. She caught a drift of smoke as if someone were burning leaves, but it was late spring, not fall.

It was Dick Arshen. Behind him, a maroon Porsche convertible held a woman in the passenger seat. She looked bent and very small.

The cloud having passed and the sun blinding her again, Helen squinted as Dick crossed the road to join her.

"Out for a morning walk?" he asked.

"Yes, and you are out for a morning drive, it seems."

She realized the burning leaves smell was Dick's pipe, that he now held his palm over in his right hand. He was wearing a green tweed jacket over a blue oxford shirt, no tie, and some gray Dockers. He looked good.

"Come meet Patsy," Dick said, throwing his arm back as if to introduce the next act of a show.

"Oh, I'd love to," Helen answered.

Together, they looked both ways, but there was no traffic. Dick took Helen's elbow and held it while they crossed the street.

"Patsy, this is Helen Baird. She was a high school friend and now she's an editor at the company. Helen, meet my bride, Patsy Arshen."

"Helen, it's so nice to meet you," Patsy said in a faltering weak voice.

He called her his bride. Helen was thinking how charming that was.

"Hello, Patsy," Helen said. "Are you enjoying these beautiful parts here?"

"Oh, yes, I am," she said. She was smiling, but Helen could tell she was in pain. She looked shriveled and far older than Dick. There was a deep line between her brows, and etched lines from her nose to her mouth, which was thin, cracked, and slightly blistered. There were dark blue hollows under her eyes, and the whites of her eyes looked yellowish. Helen knew she was ill with MS and an invalid, but she never expected Patsy Arshen was a woman so debilitated as this woman was. Helen could see she was brave, not just now on this ride, but that she had bravery in her bones. She could see that Dick loved her but knew she was no longer a real partner of his life. Loyalty and admiration were holding him to her. Suddenly she felt very sorry for both.

"We were getting cabin fever," Patsy said. "Well, I was getting cabin fever." She smiled.

"Welcome to our very country part of the country," Helen said. "What a surprise."

"A very nice surprise," Dick said.

Helen remembered her dinner party, hesitated for a few seconds, but then said:

"You know what. I'm having a very small dinner party tomorrow night, around 7. It's my first in years and years. I'd be happy if you both came."

"What a nice invitation, Helen," Patsy said. "I think Dick should come." She looked at Dick with so much love in her eyes, Helen noticed, and he looked down. He was sad, very sad.

"Helen," she said, "You'll never believe what an old poop I am, but that is just my bedtime. I hold Dick back so often, but, darling, I really would like you to go to Helen's sweet dinner party."

Helen looked at Dick. "Most welcome, Dick," she said.

Dick looked at Patsy, and his soft brown eyes became fawn-like.

"Okay, I'd be happy to come," he said. "You said 7, right?"

"Right," Helen said.

"What can he bring, Helen?"

"Nothing. No, nothing. Just come, Dick."

"Will do," he said, and walked over to his side of the Porsche and got in.

Helen called over, "Bye you two."

Patsy waved at her and said, "Delightful to see you," and Dick pulled the Porsche back onto the road and continued his drive while Helen crossed the street and rejoined her walk.

"I'll be damned," she said to herself.

She kicked a small stone ahead of her, caught up to it, and kicked it along further.

"I'll be damned," she said out loud. "Four women and four men. Perfect."

Chapter Fourteen

Helen was pleased by her menu. She'd made a beef bourguignon with egg noodles. She'd made grilled broccoli and new carrots with brown butter, mushrooms, and shallots, a sour cherry-rhubarb crisp with homemade vanilla ice cream for dessert. Carmie was bringing the salad. Helen had selected a pinot noir with dinner and a Riesling for dessert, and bought four freshly-baked French baguettes to go with the meal. Her cleaning crew had the place spotless; must make sure she sent an extra tip through the mail next week.

Her guests were all sitting around her nine-foot long Silestone island. She turned her head to look through the door into her dining room where she had planned to serve dinner. The long mahogany dining table was meticulously dressed with her mother's embroidered green table cloth, and fresh cherry blossoms from her garden were in her mother's Chinese vases. Hank's mother's two sterling candelabra stood at either end of the table, their new cream-colored candles at attention, waiting to be lit.

Dick and Fred Unger had arrived first, and they sat at the island talking while Helen tended all of her dishes on the oven top. As guests entered, they joined Dick and Fred at the island. By the time Helen got around to serving dinner, the whole party was sitting around the island. Everyone looked so comfortable, head-to-head in conversations, that Helen gave up on the dining room and served the bourguignon in two clashing sets of crockery she used for every day.

Dick tended to wine-pouring, and within an hour everyone was talking two decibels above normal pitch and at least three separate conversations were going on.

Helen noticed how nice Dick looked tonight in a blue denim shirt and pair of charcoal cotton pants. He'd asked everyone if they minded if he lit up his pipe and everyone except Janet Masland said, "Fine." She was being a pill. Throughout dinner she could only talk about her husband and how he was suffering since their daughter ran away. At first, she sat with Tom Jiang, but out of the corner of her eye, Helen saw that Tom fairly quickly excused himself and walked around to join Jared Klein. The two were interesting for Helen to watch, Tom with his Chinese-American looks, was about six feet tall, and he stood, one leg on the cross-bar of the stool, the rest of his lanky-self slouching, one hand on the island, leaning down to hear dark-haired Jared talking non-stop about something Helen could not quite hear. Good old Carmie had joined Janet for a while, no doubt because Carmie felt obligated to talk with someone in her support group. Helen saw Carmie's good right eye glass over to where it looked like her false left eye. Carmie wasn't going to last much longer with Janet. Helen would have to be the next one to take on Janet. Thankfully, shortly after dinner Janet excused herself to Helen, saying she had to get home to her husband. Gracious, but insincere, regrets were uttered on all sides, and Janet left the party before Helen served dessert or had to talk to her.

Now it was four men and three women.

Dick came over to Helen after Janet left, put his hand on her shoulder and said:

"Few things ratchet up odds that a dinner party will be pleasant more than the departure of an unpleasant guest."

"Oh, now Dick, you're being catty. Go talk to Fred Unger. He looks alone over there now that Sonia has abandoned him."

"Oh, yes, I see," Dick said, ready to do his bit so that everyone had a pleasant evening.

By now, Carmie had gone to sit next to Sonia, and the two were in an animated conversation.

Wonder what on earth those two have to talk about? Helen thought, as she moved to the sideboard to get the crisp ready to serve.

"Okay, everyone," she said, tapping her finger against her wine glass.

"Isn't she lovely," she heard Dick say to Fred, who nodded agreement.

"Lovely is as lovely does," Helen said, "and I hope I've made a dessert that pleases all of you. You know, this is my first dinner party in years, since…well since it all, and I couldn't be more pleased with my guest list."

Everyone, on various trajectories toward drunkenness said, "Here, Here, Helen."

The crisp and ice cream were well-received, and once the dessert plates were cleared from the island, folks settled into conversations they'd begun earlier, and Dick lit his pipe. A sweet smell circled through the room and, oddly, made Helen feel safe. She watched Dick smoke his pipe. His form, tall, broad yet trim was undeniably agreeable. His fawn-like eyes, deeply set in a face of just slightly olive skin pleased her. For the first time, he seemed to her to be very attractive.

He saw her look at him and came over to her.

"Nice party, Helen. Really nice."

"I wondered whether you and Sonia would feel comfortable at the same party, but, where is she?" Helen looked around. "Oh, still talking to Carmie. I guess it didn't bother her."

"Nah," Dick said. "We sometimes socialize with Sonia. She's more like a third partner at this point."

"Sorry Patsy couldn't come," Helen said.

"Nah, Patsy would never come out so late," he said.

Helen thought she'd heard a slight catch in his voice.

"Is she very ill, Dick?"

"She's dying," he said. "But she's been dying for years now."

"I'm so sorry, Dick."

"So am I. So am I. Gotta get home. Great party, Helen."

He gave her a peck on the cheek and called out to everyone:

"Night, everyone. Great seeing you all."

Helen knew that her cheek was flushed, and she wanted to throw herself back into her party, so she joined Tom and Jared who paused their conversation as she joined them.

"Well," Tom said, "better push off now. Jared, you going my way?"

"Am. And Thanks, Helen."

Suddenly Carmie and Sonia looked up. They looked like two kids who'd gotten bleary-eyed watching a movie, but in their case, it was a long and intense conversation that made them look blurry.

"Oh my God," Carmie said. "We locked the joint down."

"Oh my God," Sonia said, "Right you are."

"You both be careful driving home," Helen said. "A bit of wine tonight."

"Oh, yes, Helen," Sonia said. "Very careful."

"Yup, careful," Carmie said.

Suddenly, Helen was alone in her kitchen. She'd clean up the next morning after she'd slept to her heart's content.

Chapter Fifteen

Helen was awakened at 9 a.m. by her cell. She groaned and turned over, ignoring the phone. Ten minutes later, it was ringing again.

"Shut up!" She'd been getting hang-up calls lately. She'd rush to answer the phone, say hello, and whoever it was would click off and then call again in ten or twenty minutes.

"Hello!" she snapped.

"Hello. Is this Helen Baird."

"You mean the woman you just woke up. Yes, Helen Baird." Helen winced at how rude she was, but she just couldn't get on the sunny side of the street right out of sleep.

"Sorry I woke you, Helen. This is Paul Baird."

"Paul who?"

"Paul Baird. Your brother."

Helen was silent.

"Your brother, the criminal."

"Oh, well," Helen said, "Don't let that bother you. I'm a criminal now, too."

Paul burst out in a quick, shallow laughter.

His laugh sounded genuine, but she could tell he was nervous.

"Where are you, Paul?" She paused a minute and then added, "Are you in prison?"

Paul started laughing again. "No, no. I'm out. Finally. 26 years and 3 months, but I'm out now." His laughter erupted again, but softly. "Jeez. Never imagined this call going this way."

"Well," Helen said. "I just don't know what to say. I should have visited, Paul. I should have written you. I…I'm sorry. There's no excuse for it."

"No, problem. I know, it's a been a weird relationship or lack of we've had our whole lives."

"Yes, I know, too. I just don't know what to say to you now," Helen said. "Well, one thing. Did you really murder that guy or were you set up?"

"Could we talk about that a little later?"

"Yeah, sure. Sorry I brought it up," Helen said. "Well, do you know Mother and Dad are gone now?"

"Yup," he said. "We get that kind of news in prison. Knew that." He waited for her to say something, but she didn't. "Look, Helen. I'm calling to find out if you'd be willing to meet some time. When you're ready. No rush, but I'd like to, well, meet you."

"Right, Paul," Helen said. "We hardly know each other anymore. Well, where are you now?"

"I'm in eastern Ohio."

Helen liked the sound of his voice. It was a gentle voice, and it seemed to be a thoughtful voice. He was soft-spoken, not hard, rushed and staccato as she imagined a long-term jailbird's voice would be. Maybe it would be okay to meet him.

Again, Paul waited for her to say something, but when she didn't, he carried on, "I have a job. I work in oil and shale, mainly hauling pipes around, but it pays pretty well. I have an apartment, well, it's actually a little condo. I have a car. I guess I'm trying to say I've made a life for myself. Been out now two years and didn't want to call you until I was clear on my feet and doing okay, so that's how I am now. Would you be willing to meet me or not?"

Helen liked everything he said. She couldn't square this voice, these details with the small disruptive boy she knew growing up. He sounded like an entirely different person. Not like a murderer. "Yeah, okay," she said.

"Look, Helen, I know it's normal to be, well I guess afraid of someone like me. Convicted of murder, served over 20 years for murder, but I changed in prison, I really did."

"You'll have to tell me about that."

"Yeah, I will."

"So, what kind of meeting did you have in mind, Paul?"

"Can I be honest with you now?"

"You'd better be honest with me."

"Look, I've been working up to calling you for a while. I even called a few times and hung up when you answered because I was afraid you'd just…I don't know…not be willing to see me at all."

"Oh, so those hang-ups, were you?"

"Yeah, sorry about them. I just lost nerve at the last minute."

Helen heard a long, deep sign in the phone.

"So now here I am calling you and wanting to see you next week because I have time off from my job next week."

"Next week?" Helen thought quickly about what was on her schedule, if anything.

He paused but then began again as if he hadn't meant to pause. "Look, Helen, I'll be staying at a motel. I don't expect you to put me up, not knowing me at all, and that I'm a criminal, a former criminal."

Helen was silent.

"But then, you say you are, too." He laughed. "So, we'll have to get into that."

Her calendar was in the phone she was talking on, so she couldn't check, but she thought she had a clear week ahead. "Okay, next week," she said. "Come on Tuesday."

"Okay, Helen," Paul said softly, "and thanks."

"Thank you for calling, Paul."

When Helen hung up, she felt she was spinning. This was something she never expected. How would they be with one another? She'd told him to come on Tuesday just to take the role of big sister, to be bossy. "Come Tuesday," she'd said. "Guess that showed him who's boss." She flopped down on her pillow.

"Oh, my. Oh, my," she whispered. "I have a brother."

Chapter Sixteen

"Say that again, Paul."

Helen and Paul had been together on the appointed Tuesday since 8:30 a.m. Paul had flown in the night before and was staying at a hotel in town. He was supposed to come by Helen's at 9 a.m. but he really couldn't wait. Neither could Helen. She'd gotten up at 6 instead of 7 a.m., made a coffee cake from scratch and just walked around her kitchen, around and around that big island, until, mercifully, he rang the bell a half hour early. The two regarded each other the way cats first do, facing one another a few paces apart, first staring, and then moving slowly around, each making sure the other is at all times face forward. After they'd had coffee and Helen's cake, they began to relax a little. Helen had brought out all her photo albums and laid them out in the sitting room so when they migrated there, she showed him pictures of their parents as they aged, of Hank, of Kristen. She shocked herself by pouring out to him all the details about Kristen as if, well as if he were family.

He let her talk for the first two hours without saying much. Helen watched him as she talked. When he first stepped through the front door, she was surprised he was fairly short. A good 5'9", he wasn't any taller than she was though their father had been 6'3". He was fairer than she'd expected. For some reason, she recalled him as a brunette boy, but his hair was now sandy. *She'd have to look more closely*, she thought, to see if there was some gray streaking through his hair which made it look lighter. She was fascinated to find him so like their father, like an unfamiliar version of something you know so well. It was hard for her to pinpoint just what she was seeing. No, they didn't have the same nose or lips. But it was as if a photograph had been printed a quarter of an inch off-center.

Now into their third hour together, sitting head-to-head in the sitting room, having consumed the albums, Paul seemed to understood the tragedy of Kristen's condition.

"You know, I ran away in 6th grade," he said, his head in his hands.

"I didn't know that!"

"Yup. Ran off to the bus stop and was going to get on a bus to Port Authority. The bus was there, just idling, but the driver wouldn't let anyone on. So, up drives Dad in his big old blue Oldsmobile."

"Uh-oh."

"You're damned right, uh-oh. He honked once—really long and really loud—and I could see his scowl through the windshield. There wasn't even a question in my mind about what I would do. I just walked over to the Olds, opened the passenger side door and got in. Complete silence on the way home. Complete silence once we got home." All he said was:

"Your mother saved you food in the refrigerator. Enjoy it and then go to your room and go to bed. Tomorrow is Saturday, and you and I are going hiking. I will wake you at 7 a.m. and you'd best be ready to leave the house at 7.30."

"And that's all?"

"Pretty much. He wasn't a fellow for shouting or hitting as you know, but that hike was agonizing. It isn't what he said. It's what he didn't say."

"I don't know why I never knew that."

"You and I weren't great companions as children."

"Yes, right."

"But I said all this to say that I imagine I understand some of what Kristen felt when she started running away."

"Oh! Kristen!"

"Yes, and if I can help her work through some of this, I will."

Helen didn't say what she was thinking, which was, I'm not sure I'll allow that, Paul. Don't know you yet. But then she thought. *How many years has it been since I've had anything to say about who Kristen meets, talks to?*

Having begun to talk, Paul kept on talking, telling Helen about how he felt as a teenager and as he grew into his 20s. He talked about why he murdered the man who owed him $5000.00. He realized that Helen expected him to say he hadn't done it, or that he did it in self-defense. But he wasn't going to lie to her. He did murder that man. But what he wanted her to understand is that he didn't do it for that money. Even he thought he had, but he'd learned through reading while in prison that it had nothing to do with the money.

He had just told Helen that it had everything to do with Carl Jung's "shadow." She had, of course, read Jung in college, but she didn't quite get how he was applying Jung's concepts to his murder. That is when she said, "Say that again, Paul."

"Jung says we go through life thinking we know ourselves," Paul explained. "But each of us has a shadow, a part of ourselves that is hidden from us, a part we don't know and certainly don't recognize as ourselves. Some people never meet their shadows, but for others, like me, there can be an experience, something out of the ordinary, that triggers our shadow, that part of us that is hidden, and we can act from that shadow and do things we would never in a million years imagine we could do."

"Yeah?" Helen said, skeptically. She was so hoping he wasn't going to turn everything around and start playing the victim.

"Now for me, I was on a bad path from when I was little."

"Yeah, I know, Paul!" Helen said, remembering how Paul and his cronies would shoot arrows at stray dogs. "It was pretty bad, Paul when you and your friends shot arrows at dogs."

"It was," Paul said, "I lacked all moral compass, and I was wrong to stay there and watch it. I didn't shoot any arrows. The older guys did, but I'm guilty in staying to watch it."

"What about the old lady, Paul?" Helen wanted to go right down the line of what always considered crimes and hear him out, unsure now of how she would end up seeing him at the end of the day.

"Right. When she walked in, I got afraid, and I slugged her in the gut. I didn't have a concept of hurting her but I should have. I don't know why I didn't develop a real conscience until it was too late, until I'd done all these hurtful things and couldn't undo them. All I could do is think and read and try to figure out why I had no conscience then. I got a lot help to start with. We had counselors, and one of them, Tim Froan was a great guy. God, he spent so much time with me. Gave me books to read about understanding yourself. Mainly he talked with me any time I wanted to talk. Then he left after a few years. To get married and move somewhere else. It just killed me to see him go, but then I remember he always said, 'Paul, you'll find me in a book. Just look.'"

"Well, he sounds like a life-saver, literally. But something bothers me, Paul."

"What?"

"Aren't you justifying these acts, Paul?"

"Yes, I am, but in a way that is honest. I am telling you what my perspective at the time of these acts was, as cleanly as I know them myself. I'm not trying to get out of anything because I've been convicted, judged by all these acts, and I have accepted the consequences and know they were deserved. But I want you to know as clearly as I do what was in my mind at the time."

"Go on, Paul."

"That murder was something totally different from my earlier crimes. I went to have a talk with that guy. It got heated and then he hit me, pardon me, in the balls with his knee so hard that I saw stars. Literally saw stars. What reached out of me then were my two hands, which I admit strangled him, but what really reached out of me that day was my shadow. I felt then that I was someone else. I mean, I knew I was me, but I also knew a force in me that I'd never known before was controlling me."

"Humm," Helen said.

"This is not a way to excuse what I did. I'm on the other side of 26 years and 3 months of incarceration for that crime—it was a crime—and I deserved to lose 25 years and 3 months of my life or more for taking another life. But what I'm saying is that when I strangled that man, it was the shadow in me reaching out and controlling me. I have that understanding of my crime."

"Got to think through all this, Paul," Helen said.

"I know," Paul said. "You may decide you want nothing to do with me. That's the chance I knew I'd take in coming to see you. Anyway, everything I've told you today is something I've never told anyone else, but I want you to hear how I've come to think about all this."

Helen smiled at him.

"You're my sister," he said.

Helen let him kiss her on her cheek when he left for the motel. She liked him. She thought she believed him. There was nothing shady about him that she could see. It was pretty clear he wanted her in his life. She'd have to process all this before she'd know if she, too, wanted him in her life.

Chapter Seventeen

Helen thought about Paul's visit all week. She was glad she had it to think about because it made this day come faster.

Following Minnie's advice to take Helen into the City with her, Carmie had called the week before to say it was this day, this Saturday that she and Helen would go into the City even though it had been rainy all week. Carmie had word that Kristen and Jamal were usually out on Saturday mornings and walked several blocks together to a CTown Supermarket and back. It was still dark, but Helen was up and walking around in her house to calm her nerves.

Both happy and horrible thoughts were stirring through Helen's mind as she found the socks she wanted to wear and then changed her mind and got a different pair. She ran to her full-length mirror to see how her socks looked.

"For Pete's sake," she said loudly. There she stood in her underwear and red socks.

"Carmie said camouflage."

The pair of red socks, by far her most comfortable pair, came off for black ones.

Helen had been dawdling over her socks and thinking about her party when she noticed the clock said 5:55 a.m. Carmie would honk at 6 a.m. sharp. Helen went into speed-dial, putting on what she'd laid out the night before, and by 6 a.m. she was at her front door, watching out the side window in the door for Carmie's old VW bus.

The VW's engine was loud, so Helen heard Carmie a block away, locked her door, and ran down to the curb. She jumped into the VW bus before Carmie even came to a full stop.

"Whoa there, Helen," Carmie said. "It's going to be a long day that needs a lot of patience."

"Got it," Helen said, handing Carmie a piece of the apple bread she had in her frig.

"Oh, yum," Carmie said and finished the bread in three bites. Crumbs spilled down the front of Carmie's dark blue shirt to the floor, adding to the overall dishevelment of the bus with its stacks of magazines on the passenger side floor.

"Just kick them over," Carmie said.

"Maybe I can put them in the back of the van?"

"Yeah, sure."

Used cans of soda rested on seats in the back, each folded neatly in half.

"Did you do that, Carmie?" Helen asked when she saw them all sitting like open books.

"Oh, yeah," Carmie said. "Got to keep my muscle tone while living with all those nuns," she said.

"Do you really plan to leave the sisterhood?" Helen began.

"They like to gather and chat about God, and I don't. I do action. Haven't fully decided yet, but I sure am leaning toward it."

"What would you do?"

"Move out!" Carmie laughed. "I'd probably be able to keep my ministry. No one else could do it, and you've seen what a need there is."

"A huge need."

"So, then I'd just renounce my religious vows, set up the ministry as a charitable group, write a grant for funding, and away we go. Father Finnegan is very cool. He'll help me. He can't stand these old nuns either."

"Where would you live?"

"That," Carmie paused almost as if there was a laugh in her voice, "remains to be seen at the moment."

"What does that mean?" Helen asked.

"It means what it says. It means we'll see in time."

Helen was getting irritated again with Carmie, the way she'd been before she went into the City to look for Kristen by herself. She shrugged off Carmie's enigmatic answers and concentrated on how good Carmie was to be driving Helen in to look for Kristen.

"Oh, so, hey," Helen said, "did you enjoy the party?"

"So, so much, Helen." Carmie smiled. "You have no idea."

"What does that mean?"

"Means I had a hell of a good time."

"Okay, I'm not going to talk to you until you decide to stop talking in tongues."

They were still on dark and winding country roads with no one else around, but they could see the lights of the town ahead where they'd pick up the highway junction into the City.

"Look, Helen," Carmie said. "I'm a good driver, but I'm still a bit shaky, so if you wouldn't mind not talking, I'll do a lot better."

"Oh," Helen said. "I know all about it. Sure thing."

Carmie cast a tight-mouthed glare Helen's way.

Helen pushed her seat back and reclined it. This request for silence might mean she could doze off, and she closed her eyes. It was dark, and the passing street lights made a kaleidoscope of images on her inner eyelid, and she found the effect dizzying, but she liked it. She kept watching her inner eyelids with closed eyes. She thought of Hank, but she blocked that thought. Dick came to mind. She was stunned that she felt an attraction to him. When they were in high school, she didn't think he was sexy. But now. He'd filled out and his sexuality was low-key and appealing. She wondered what his relationship with Patsy was like. She couldn't imagine him with someone so ill and needy, yet he obviously loved her deeply. *They must have been crazy in love when they were younger,* she thought, *and they must be doing their best to be there for each other during what Dick implied was her final illness.*

"I wonder if he'll call," Helen said drowsily.

Carmie shot her a glance.

"Oh, sorry, Carmie," Helen said, jolting awake. "I talked."

The bus took a wide swerve to the right and then a sharp pull to the left. Helen watched as Carmie passed a car on the right and jacked the steering wheel hard to the left to get back in the lane for the juncture to Route 80 East.

Helen's eyes bulged, but she said nothing. Carmie turned her head to find the juncture, and Helen could see Carmie's one eye rimmed with concentration while the other staid glass eye remained torpid.

Carmie grunted as she wheeled the van around others, doing at least 75.

Helen wanted with all her might to say, "Are we in a hurry, Carmie?" but she could see Carmie's intense concentration in the steel-rod stiffness of her forearms as she grasped the steering wheel, so Helen maintained silence. She kept looking around for the police siren, for she was sure they'd be stopped on the highway.

Carmie's tense forearm navigation soon had them on the upper level of the George Washington Bridge.

Helen grabbed the window handle. Who in the world takes the upper level?

The orange and white VW bus bounced through the exit ramps, tossing Helen's knees into the glove compartment once, and after some raucous right and left turns, they were suddenly on Broadway.

Carmie got herself in the right lane and slowed to about 30 mph.

"Okay, Helen," she said. "You can talk."

Helen was concentrating on breathing, but after a few seconds, said, "So now what do we do?"

"Now we cruise, Helen. Eyes right and left, and when we get down into the fifties, we turn around and cruise north to the nineties and then we turn around again and cruise south."

"But I thought you had info on where they go on Saturday mornings."

Carmie shot Helen a sharp angry glance, "I do, so you want me to go and park in front of the CTown, for Christ's sake? Some kind of spy you'd make, Helen."

Helen wanted to snap back, but she let it go.

"Just wondering why our radius is so wide," she said.

"People don't always do what they usually do," Carmie said. "So cast a wide net, and you are more likely to catch a fish."

"Oh, now I see," Helen said, grinning to herself.

They were driving so slowly in the right lane going south that it almost seemed as if the few early morning risers on the streets were walking in slow motion. Carmie had slowed to about 15 mph as she perused the south side sidewalk. She could get away with this because besides delivery trucks and some cabs in the middle and left lanes, the roads were fairly empty. Helen watched out her right window as they drove parallel to a man about sixty trudging along, holding a pail that looked like lunch. They kept pace with him so well that she thought she could lean out the window and ask him what he was having for lunch.

"How long before we see them, Carmie?"

"Be what it will be, Helen,"

They reached the mid-fifties, and Carmie said, "Okay, Helen, we'll wheel around and head back north."

Helen thought how long it had been since she'd lived with Kristen. She wasn't the Kristen she knew after she got sick. How much more was she likely to have changed? How sick was she now? Did she take any medication other than birth control pills? Helen watched the northbound sidewalk closely. They saw several people waiting at bus stops and others running to them, but Kristen wasn't among them.

"Okay, Helen, turning south again," Carmie said as she made an illegal U-turn in the nineties.

They prowled through the nineties and into the eighties like a big cat moving one sure foot slowly ahead of the other, quietly, firmly, slowly, and stealthily.

"There," Carmie said softly. She pointed down 86th street at what looked like a dim hump to Helen.

Carmie slowed the van to a walk and then she stopped it near the curb once it crossed 86th street.

"Look back, Helen. I think it's them from when I saw them before. But do not lean out the window and do not say one thing, Helen, or they'll run."

"How can you tell. It's still dark, and all this rain is making it darker."

"Just look and for God's sake, shut up."

Helen turned her whole body around, so she was facing her seat back. She looked out the back of the bus as her eyes adjusted to the dim light. The hump was still in the distance, but she could tell it was a male and female, arms around each other tightly. They were under an umbrella, and he kept looking at her as if to make sure she was okay. She had on what looked like layers of tops that flopped this way and that on her body as the wind picked up. They walked very slowly and carefully down the slippery sidewalk. The male stepped out in front and held out his hand to help the girl across a puddle. *Just like Sir Walter Raleigh,* Helen thought. They were coming closer, and Helen could see glints of light across their faces from the street lights above. Helen looked only at the girl. She could see a front wave flapping across the girl's forehead. It waved just like Kristen's hair. As the girl got closer, Helen knew it was Kristen because of her slightly pigeon-toed walk. They got closer and closer and when they were two stores away, Helen gasped.

"Oh, my God, my God. It's Kristen," Helen whispered over and over.

"Shut up, Helen. For God's sake, shut up," Carmie whispered.

The couple looked calm as they took mincing steps across puddles, getting closer and closer. They were now walking in the light the CVS store threw onto the sidewalk, and Helen saw that Kristen looked happy and that the young man looked smitten with her. Helen studied his face for a moment. He looked kind, steady, bright, and caring. *And he's handsome*, Helen thought.

The couple hit a dry patch under the CVS awning and picked up their walking pace slightly. They were almost at the back of the VW bus.

"Won't they recognize your bus?" Helen whispered.

"Maybe, but they won't know you're in it if you stay down and shut up."

Helen looked up over her back seat just as they were passing the bus. She saw them stand, waiting at the curb while the pedestrian sign flashed red.

The girl looked back over her shoulder and stepped toward the bus.

She called out, "Hi, Mom," and held up her middle finger directed at the van. "And don't ever chase me down a street again!" she shouted.

The pedestrian sign flashed green.

The boy took Kristen's other hand and tugged her forward.

"Come on, Kristen," he said gently.

Chapter Eighteen

The whole ride home, Helen's eyes were half shut and puffy. She cried more from shock than sadness that her daughter had given her the finger.

"What could I possibly have done, Carmie?"

"You mean good or bad?"

Helen shot at glance at Carmie, whose face was pinched into a beady-eyed stare at the traffic in front of her. For as much driving back and forth to the City that Carmie did, she hated driving. She hunched over the steering wheel and jerked her feet from the gas to the brake pedal, never sure which one it should be.

Helen slumped down and rested her head against her seat. There was no point talking to Carmie while she was driving.

"Good or bad?" Carmie asked again.

"Turn on the radio, won't you, Carmie. Something classical. I'm just beyond everything right now and will just rest my eyes while you drive."

Carmie turned the radio on pre-set to an all-news channel.

Helen sat forward to change the channel but then slumped back again.

"I'll listen to their words instead of mine," she said.

"Makes sense," Carmie said, slamming her foot on the brake. "God damn it," she yelled. She then pushed the accelerator pedal down hard, passed the driver in front of her, quickly rolled down her window and screamed out the window, "Learn to drive the damn thing, Bimbo!"

"Good grief, Carmie! You're not allowed to say 'God Damn it,' are you?"

"Who's listening?" Carmie said.

"I am," Helen said.

"Yeah, you who can't decide if she did good or bad, so what's the difference what I say in the privacy of this car?"

"Aren't there nun rules about such things?"

"You just spend a day in that house with those bitches," Carmie grimaced, "I'll show you nun rules. Ha!"

"Hey, and also, how did you get a driver's license with a glass eye?"

"I didn't," Carmie said.

"What! Then why are we bouncing around in this orange VW bus?"

"You don't think I know how to outfox any cop who'd try to come after me? Really, Helen!"

"You shock me, Carmie," Helen said.

"You shock me, too, Helen."

"How in hell do I shock you?"

"By wondering if you did good or bad," Carmie said. "You did the best you knew how. There was some good in that and some bad. That's all there is to it."

Helen wept again.

"Oh, come on, Helen," Carmie said, reaching her hand over to Helen's. "Nothing's promised in this life. Nothing at all, and you don't know what's going to be. You just have to live with that."

Helen tried not to cry for the rest of the ride. She closed her eyes. The sun was up and breaking through some clouds, so Helen watched the patterns the sun and trees were making on the inside of her eyelids as Carmie rambled over bridges, on highways, and through back roads until she reached Helen's house.

"We're here," Carmie called out, thinking she was waking Helen. "We'll talk through all this in a few days."

"Right. Ah to sleep the rest of the day away," Helen said.

"Buck up!" Carmie said, revving her accelerator several times to signal her readiness to get going.

Helen didn't sleep the day away, just most of it.

Chapter Nineteen

Instead of sleeping, Helen kept seeing Kristen's obscene gesture and thought about all the destruction Kristen's illness had caused in her life. Some people at Carmie's support group, if they were forward enough, crass enough, or brave enough sometimes asked Helen about being the mother of a runaway. They were new to this, and they wanted to know what it was like to be the mother of a child who had run away and rejected her. She said she was like a pressure cooker boiling over. They asked her more questions, but she just said, "That's all."

She hadn't thought what it was like for Hank when she refused to talk to him about her immeasurable grief. Her mourning for the loss of their child that she had known had made Helen selfish. She could not share her sorrow. She believed if she opened herself to Hank, the sorrow would swallow her. She thought if she launched into a telling of it, she would never stop, but just go down a deep hole with it. Like Eurydice, she'd fall into hell, and Hank was not Orpheus-enough to save her.

Yet one night, he tried to be by taking Helen out to dinner to remind her she was strong and beautiful.

***

"Go buy a really expensive dress," Hank had said. "And we'll throw it out after dinner!"

Helen had put on make-up for the first time in a few years.

They drove thirty miles to The Hatfield House, the best restaurant around, and Helen ordered Blood Orange Cobia with capers. Hank ordered red snapper and a Louis Jadot Chassagne at eighty-five dollars a bottle. Little white twinkly lights all around the ceiling momentarily cheered Helen, but right after the waiter left to put their order in, Helen found tears on her cheeks, and then her eyes opened like a dike along a roaring river, and she could not stop. She bowed her head behind her napkin when the waiter brought their dinner.

"Like the cobia?" Hank tried to bring her back to him.

"Oh, it's good, real good. It's just. Hank, this is so hard."

"I know it is, Helen. We just have to do the best we can. That's all we can do."

"Yes, of course." She ate several bites in between sharp in-takes of breath to stop the tears, but she couldn't stop them.

"Want to try my red snapper?" Hank tried once more.

Helen pushed her plate away from her. "Can't eat anymore."

When the bill came, she realized that the people at nearby tables knew she'd had some sort of break-down right there over her Blood Orange cobia. As she and Hank got up to leave, they all bowed their heads until she'd passed by.

At that dinner, Helen's darkest thoughts surfaced and made her heart confront the loss of Kristen, at least, losing the child she bore, with the traits and potential she knew. There was another person there instead, one foreign to her.

It was raining when she and Hank left the Hatfield House. She took his arm, and he put up the umbrella.

"I don't know who is in Kristen's body," she wept.

"It's Kristen, an irreversibly infected Kristen."

"But I miss her."

"I know, darling. I know." Hank squeezed her hand in his.

"When Kristen was eighteen and first ran away to that town square where she slept on benches at night, I brought her a hot meal every day."

"I know you did, darling."

"I could find her because of her hat, remember that hat, Hank?"

He'd heard these stories a hundred times before, either from Helen or in his own head; it's

the nature of a tragedy as great as theirs. It repeats, endlessly repeats in the minds of those who suffered it.

They had one more block before they'd reach their car.

"Then I made a huge mistake. I asked her, 'Kristen, why are you here. Come home, please.'"

"I came the next day, but she was gone. Just gone."

Hank would have done anything to change the conversation, but he knew Helen needed to tell this story yet again.

He said, "That's when we didn't see her for two weeks and then she just showed up in the kitchen one day."

"Yes, you're right, and she was dirty, cold, and hungry, and I'll never forget the hard look in her eyes when she said, 'I'm here, yeah, so what. Just for today. I need food."

"I never knew why she ran off after that," Hank added.

"I yelled at her for leaving the mayonnaise out. She left it on the counter all day, and it went bad. What a fool I was!"

"No, don't, Helen."

"It is my fault," she said and fell silent.

They reached their car.

"Cooler tonight," Hank commented.

"Then after Kristen left that time, that was it. Then I saw a flimsy paper notice tacked to a tree in town advertising Carmie's support groups. I got a little hope. Remember how much hope I had then, Hankie?"

Helen looked at Hank. He was quietly humming along to a Credence Clearwater song on the radio.

Story-time was over; chance things like Borrelia burgdorferi and a hand-written notice tacked to a maple tree, the things that matter in life that you can't talk about.

***

What was it like to be so sick over your daughter's rejection of you?

The answer is the questions in Helen's mind the night Hank took her to dinner and the day Kristen gave her the finger because they were the same questions. Who was Kristen these days? Was Helen her mother any longer? What would it be like to try to be a mother to this strange and unpleasant young woman? Would she get all caught up in Kristen's life again and try to save her while losing herself? These memories of losing pieces of herself, almost as surely as she'd lost pieces of Kristen were vivid, and she wanted to get away from this dismal mood that had engulfed her. Her cell was against her thigh, so when it rang, she answered it on the first ring.

"And what are you doing tonight, Helen?" It was Dick.

"Oh," she said.

"Did I interrupt a nap?"

"Yes, as a matter of fact."

"Well what about getting some really good Italian food with me tonight. Nothing fancy. Just in Symington. A great place there called *Prego.*"

"With you and Patsy?"

"Patsy is already asleep, but she said to tell you she would have liked to join us."

Helen had imagined her evening drooping around her house, maybe crying some, and something in her rebelled against that.

"When are you picking me up?" she said.

Chapter Twenty

Prego charmed Helen. It was small with red, green, and white lights all over the walls.

"Italian flag in lights," Dick said when they walked in.

The tables and chairs were knotty pine, and instead of a small vase of half-dead flowers crowding the tables, pewter chains hung from the ceiling about five feet above the middle of each table. Pots in a red, green, and white mosaic pattern hung from the chains and held overflowing ivy plants. The ambiance of the room made people want to eat and drink well.

Both Helen and Dick felt like having pasta. Dick had strangozzi al tartufo nero, a thick form of spaghetti in a simple butter sauce with shavings of black truffles, and Helen, linguine all'aragosta o all'astice, linguine with lobster. Dick ordered two bottles of Far Niente Chardonnay right from the start, so the two had loosened up even before their meals arrived.

After dinner, Dick reached over and put his hand over Helen's hand, resting in a curve, on top of the table.

"Dick. What are you doing?"

"I'm feeling your warmth, Helen. That's what."

"Not appropriate," Helen said, lifting her hand and moving the salt and pepper cellars to the side of the table. Dick put his hand back on the table.

"Why not."

"You're married," she said, brushing back a thin strand of hair that had fallen across her face.

He smiled to himself, shook his head softly and said:

"You think with Patsy in the shape she's in, I haven't, well, had lady friends?"

"How could you do that to Patsy! She is such a sweet woman," Helen said, affronted. The strand again fell into her face and she, again, pushed it back.

"She is the sweetest woman alive," Dick said, "and I love her. I love her dearly."

Helen looked straight into his eyes, stunned by what he said.

"Look, Helen. I'll always love Patsy, and she knows it. She hasn't been up to any intimacy for more than ten years. She pulled me aside one day and told me to do what I needed to do, that it was fine with her if I had intimate relations, as she put it, with ladies—also her word—because she no longer had the stamina for it." Dick drummed the fingers of his right hand softly on the table.

"My goodness," Helen muttered, sitting straight in her chair.

"So, don't think Patsy doesn't know I've been intimate with other women?"

"You tell her?" Helen's back was stiff.

"Of course not! But she knows. She's just that selfless She says she's robbed me of a man's need for intimacy."

"Sex," Helen interjected. Her fingers passed down the creases of her lips as if to remove excess lipstick in the corners.

"Same thing," Dick said, "and she's given me her blessing to have whatever kind of relationships I want to have."

Helen was still and listening intently. "But if you're with someone else, who looks after her?" she questioned. "Doesn't she get lonely?"

"Her sister's been living with us for three years. The two of them gab all day. Sometimes I think Patsy would like me to move out and just let her and her sister be." He bowed his head. "She's my little bride, but she just couldn't go the whole way."

Helen saw tears fill Dick's right eye, but he blinked them back.

"So, lovely Helen. I'll never push you to anything. Got my word on that. But I really like you. And I find you attractive in so many ways. I'm just saying I'm open to anything with you."

Helen felt her cheeks go red, and she bowed her head.

"Didn't mean to put you on the spot, Helen. Just wanted to be out in the open."

Helen couldn't find her words. She wanted to say, how dare you! But then she realized, she had the same thoughts that Dick had. Then, what came to mind was, I love the way I could just crawl inside your tweed jacket and rest there all night. "Let's go," she finally said.

Dick's car was three blocks away, and as they walked up the street in that direction, he said, "Mind if I light my pipe?"

"Not at all," she said.

He stopped walking and reached into his pocket to get the pipe and tobacco pouch.

Helen walked a step ahead and turned, facing him. She loved seeing a man light a pipe. Her father occasionally smoked a pipe, but not like Dick, an inveterate pipe smoker. Dick lit it and puffed three or four times. That smell, that musky sweet Virginia tobacco odor surrounded Helen. She grabbed his forearms and brought him to her so that she could smell the tobacco interwoven with the tweed of his jacket. He barely had time to get his pipe out of his mouth before her lips brushed his gently, and she swept her tongue up to his right ear, taking the lobe in her mouth and teasingly suckling it. She pulled her face away for a moment and looked in his eyes.

Yes, he wanted her.

She focused on two dark flecks in his right iris that looked like planets circling an orb, but then quickly looked down at the slightly purple lip line and the plump bulging barely beige lips. She took his cheeks in her hands ever so gently and laid her lips on his. She moved her tongue slowly over both upper and lower lip and made her tongue pointed so that it slipped between his lips. His mouth opened to let her in, and she felt his tongue with her tongue, touching, flicking. She tasted the wine and Virginia leaf on his tongue and softly sucked him closer to her, and they were, finally, drinking one another deeply. Then she pulled from the kiss, and Dick held her at arms' length and looked at her a bit the way she'd seen him look at Patsy the other day.

"Helen, Helen, Helen," he said.

"Don't hold me to it," she said, slightly drunkenly.

Chapter Twenty-One

Not that Helen didn't want to see Dick. *I do*, she thought, as she passed the second block of her walk into town the morning after their dinner. She was just paralyzed about seeing him. He had asked her to have dinner with him again on Tuesday. He'd earlier mentioned that he often worked from home on Wednesdays to split up the week. She wasn't sure whether he picked Tuesday night because of this. She hadn't said yes or no to him but told him to call her. She was surprised these thoughts pushed aside thoughts of Kristen. She'd think about Kristen's middle finger, feel the well of tears, then suddenly she'd hear Dick's voice, as he talked about Patsy, as he talked about her, and she'd feel the corner of her mouth turn up in a half-smile she couldn't control.

"Morning," Helen said to the woman she passed on the sidewalk.

Once past the lady, Helen started silently rebuking herself.

What. Are you a teenager who can't wait to get male attention?

And then defend herself.

Well, what's wrong with that?

Carmie's words from the day before came back to her. "There's some good, and some bad. That's that."

She could say whatever she said to herself, but she knew another reason she was feeling reluctant to see Dick again was that they were on the brink of having sex. She could no longer imagine herself the sexual partner of anyone because of fairly recent changes in her body. She was at least twenty pounds heavier than she was five years ago.

She heard an inner voice say, what does that matter?

Then she saw the shadow of her hips elongated on the sidewalk.

Distorted by shadows, they seemed out of the question to Helen.

She saw the bounce of her hips, widened over the decades, as her walking seemed to splash them left, then right. They seemed to ripple as her shadow progressed down the sidewalk.

Oh, God. I can never be naked with any man again with these hips.

And what about her ass? She recalled that Dick was an ass man and how he'd loved to fondle and pat her behind Hank had been a breast man, so Helen had focused more on keeping her breasts high and firm for thirty-two years.

Oh, Lord! He'll go right for my ass, and it's dimpled now!

Whoa, Nellie! She said to herself.

She saw a man about two blocks ahead jogging toward her, and all Helen could think about were her jiggling hips.

I wish there were no men in the world, she thought.

The next few days, her words to herself were, this is crazy, it's all just crazy. She was a little giddy, knowing that Dick would call soon to confirm Tuesday. Then sadness about Kristen came through her giddiness like a lasso thrown around her feet from under a curtain, and she plummeted into darkness.

On Tuesday, the phone rang around noon. It was Dick, and they decided together that he'd pick up some Bluepoint oysters and clams on Tuesday and come over around 6 p.m. They'd argued about whether he should get littleneck or steamer clams. He yielded to Helen's choice of littleneck right before he said:

"Should I bring vodka? Got to eat oysters and clams with vodka."

It was then she knew they'd make love that night.

Chapter Twenty-Two

At ten before seven, there was a knock on her door. Three jaunty knocks.

There's a doorbell right there, she thought. Somehow knocking on her front door instead of using the door bell was an act of intimacy.

She passed her hands down the black dress she'd put on after thinking it made her feel a little slimmer through the hips.

Helen was just about to open the door when she saw the golden round orb of her door handle turning. Dick was opening her door from the outside.

What nerve.

Suddenly Dick was standing in front of her holding a very large bouquet of flowers.

"Helen." Dick smiled. "Look at you. You look wonderful."

"Yeah, and you're a good liar," she said before she'd approved these words coming out of her mouth.

Dick cocked his head in obvious disappointment at her reaction.

Helen's hands fluttered, and she tried to compose herself. She was so nervous she thought she might stutter.

"Open the wine," she said. She looked into his face for the first time. "Please."

Dick had dark circles under his eyes as if he'd had trouble sleeping.

She wondered if Patsy had been ill and up during the night, and he had nursed her back to sleep. She turned to walk across the room to get the wine from the refrigerator, and as she turned, she caught a glance of his midriff. He had a little bulge in front which hung slightly over his brown leather belt. Grabbing the wine, she headed back to him and handed him the wine to open.

Well he's had a good look at my ass, so if he wants to leave, he can do so right after dinner.

"Helen," he took her chin in his pointer and index fingers. "Why are you so nervous?"

"Because we're going to make love tonight," she blurted. She turned her blushing face aside, away from his fingers, thinking, tonight I have no impulse control. She winced at her words.

Dick leaned into her and kissed her.

"You were sexy in high school, and you are a new kind of sexy now, Helen."

It was as if she'd been a deflated balloon before he said these words. She could feel herself filling, even puffing up, second by second. She remembered how he'd made her feel all those years ago. She felt like a queen then.

"Come." She led Dick up the stairs to her airy bedroom with its high ceilings.

They were free with one another. Dick made Helen feel immensely attractive. She moved her hips as if she were eighteen, and Dick grabbed them as if she were. She became unselfconscious and thought for a second or two of Hank, not nostalgically but more to reflect that she felt so much more fluid with Dick.

After they made love, they went downstairs, drank vodka and ate oysters and clams and talked until early the next morning. Helen asked about Patsy, and Dick said he'd already called her. She knew where he was.

Then they slept deeply for many hours.

When Helen woke late in the day, she thought she was in bed with Hank and turned to him. When she saw half of Dick's dark hair, the rest of him burrowed under the quilt, she quietly gasped. She woke fully and just stared at Dick for several moments. *It's what I have now*, she thought. So outside of the lines I've always lived in, but it's here now.

Chapter Twenty-Three

Dick and Helen were still in bed when Carmie dropped by, unannounced as always. When Helen heard the loud banging at the door and Carmie calling out, "It's Carmie," she put on her bathrobe and ran downstairs.

Carmie told Helen she had a message for her from Kristen.

Helen, all thumbs, fixed tea for Carmie as she always did, while her mind screamed, What? Just call out the message. Just tell me, Carmie, now. When she brought the tea out on a tray, she said, "So, did you bring another obscene gesture from my daughter for me?"

"No, Helen. Sit down, and let's talk."

"Is she still with that boy, what's his name, Jamal?" Helen handed Carmie her tea.

Just then they both heard a loud bang from the ceiling.

Carmie looked at Helen.

"I have a guest," Helen said.

"Good for you," Carmie said.

Helen took a sip of tea.

"The message?" she asked, sitting closer to Carmie.

"Kristen wants to meet with you."

"What?"

"Soon," Carmie said. She looked up to the ceiling. "Just you and me."

"Yes, yes, yes," Helen said.

"Where, when?"

"She suggested meeting in Manhattan."

"That's fine," Helen said. "Oh, Carmie," she reached over and hugged Carmie. "Anything's fine. You know that."

"Now be still, Helen." Carmie detached from their embrace and put her hands on Helen's shoulders. "You don't know, and I don't know what her message is. Just that she wants to meet with you."

"Yes, yes, I know," Helen said. She felt so giddy. "But can you even imagine this? Can you see how unreal this is after all these years of her running away, literally running away."

"Well, she'd like us both to come into the City and meet at a coffee shop on 72nd and Broadway, and Jamal would be there."

"They sound serious…like a couple, Carmie."

"I think they are, but we'll see on Saturday. Now don't think any thoughts."

Helen put a huge frown on her face. "You're asking the impossible now, Carmie?"

"Well, I can see you're excited, Helen, but what if she says they're going to move to California?"

"Why would they do that?"

"I'm not saying they would, but you got to be ready for any message."

"If they were going to move to California, they'd just do it. Not like she's given me an itinerary of her movements up to now."

Helen got up and circled around the sofa. Then she sat back down. "No, it's got to be some message that has to do with me."

"Maybe she wants to rail at you for all her troubles. It may not be pleasant, Helen."

"Then at least I'll know what's on her mind. I can deal with it."

"Can you? What if it's about Hank?"

Helen's head lurched forward slightly.

"What about Hank?"

"I don't know. She might be angry you sent me to tell her about his death."

Helen blinked back welled tears. "I couldn't ask you then, but how did she take it?"

"Nothing."

"Nothing?"

"Nothing in front of me. Stoic. More like blank than stoic. She just said thanks and went over to a friend. They walked off together."

"Okay, Carmie, I've got it. I'm not to imagine this or that. I just have to walk into it blindly."

"Atta girl, Helen. You're seeing it now."

Chapter Twenty-Four

"Where are these young ones?" Carmie yawned.

Carmie and Helen sat side by side in a corner booth at the appointed coffee shop at 9 a.m. It was one of those unseasonably cool, rainy, clammy days that rarely come in summer. Helen kept sipping her water through a straw to have something to do while she waited to meet with her daughter for the first time in years.

"So glad they had fresh lemons for my water." She turned to Carmie.

"That cannot be where your head is right now," Carmie said.

"It isn't," Helen said, "and by the way, you are the grumpiest nun I've ever known."

"Then you've led a protected life." Carmie laughed.

"Any closer to a decision, Carmie?"

"Yeah, I'm leaving in a month."

"Really?"

"Really!" Carmie said. "Then life can begin."

"What does life look like for you after all this?"

"State secrets! So here we are. Aren't your thoughts on your daughter?"

"They can't be, Carmie," Helen sipped her water. "It's a survival skill I learned in therapy. Got to keep my thoughts on me in the moment." Helen's eyes teared up. "There's an alternate life just waiting for me." She looked at Carmie, hoping that would stop her tearing, but it made it worse. "It's a life where I lose my mind and never stop weeping. And it's so close I can feel it and taste the tears from it. Unless I am strict with myself when thoughts come, it's right there with long arms to reach out and possess me. If it does that, I don't return, Carmie."

"Oh, Helen," Carmie reached her right arm around Helen and pulled her close. "I get it. I get it."

Helen burrowed her head in the shoulder of Carmie's big Army-green surplus cotton shirt and let a few tears escape along with a deep and ragged cry.

"Crying again?"

Helen reared her head back at the sound of that voice.

Kristen and Jamal were standing beside the booth. Jamal had his arm around Kristen and a worried look in his soft brown eyes. Kristen stood rigidly, yet she kept herself close to him, disdain oozing from her eyes.

"Kristen!" Helen said and reached out for her hand.

Kristen put her hand in her pocket.

"Can we sit down?" she asked.

"Of course," Helen said, gesturing to the other side of their booth. "Would you introduce your friend to us?"

"This isn't my friend. He's my lover," Kristen said unceremoniously as she slid into the booth.

Then she turned to Jamal, "You must be thinking Holy Shit, what am I doing sitting here with a bunch of white people."

Carmie's head bounced forward slightly, showing her shock at how uncomfortable Kristen was making them all.

Helen watched Jamal closely. Yes, she saw a flicker of that thought pass through his eyes.

"Kristen," Jamal said softly, meant only for her ears, "there are better ways."

Kristen looked lovingly at Jamal. She reached her hand up and placed it on his cheek. Then she leaned into him and kissed his cheek. He slid closer to her and kissed her cheek.

This gave Helen time to look Jamal over. He was a handsome man, about six feet, soft brown skin, symmetrical features on a face that emanated intelligence. He looked to be almost thirty. She felt ashamed to be wondering what he was doing with Kristen who struck her now as a spoiled girl with a scowl and a sour expression. She had always been more cute than beautiful, but now she was neither because of her expression. All of Helen's longing to have Kristen back in her life was chased back by her daughter's manners and affect like a wave chased back into the ocean after cresting on shore. She turned from Kristen to Jamal. She was forming a good impression of him, partly because he exuded kindness and intelligence but also because she could see his affection for Kristen and how gently he treated her.

"Hello, Sister," Kristen said.

"Kristen," Carmie said. "Look, just call me Carmie."

"Fine," Kristen said shortly.

Jamal reached his hand across the table and shook the hand Carmie extended.

"Thank you, Carmie, for the work you do. You've helped a lot of kids, ah, people," Jamal said.

"Thank you, Jamal, and bless you," Carmie squeezed his hand.

"What can I get you?" A thirty-something waitress with brittle blonde hair was at the side of the booth.

"I'll have tea," Kristen said, "Earl Gray with two teaspoons of honey."

"Same as always!" Helen smiled at Kristen, who looked away.

Carmie and Helen each ordered another coffee, and Jamal asked only for water.

"So," Carmie said, taking control of the conversation. "You wanted to meet, Kristen?" she asked.

Kristen looked at Jamal, hoping he would speak, but he put out his hand in a gesture that invited Kristen to talk.

The waitress returned with the coffees and water. "Tea in a minute," she said.

In the respite that stirring sugar into coffee afforded, Kristen's expression changed from sour to fearful. As soon as the waitress left, she looked at her mother.

"Jamal and I would like to move in with you for a while."

Helen put her hand to her chest. Carmie swung her head to look at Helen's reaction.

"Well, I," Helen stammered. "Well, yes, of course, yes. We'll have to work out the how it will all look in the house, but of course, yes."

Jamal looked at Kristen so intently that Helen and Carmie stared at him looking at her.

Kristen glanced at him, acknowledging whatever message he was trying to convey.

"There is a reason," Kristen said. "A good reason. A very special reason we're asking this." Kristen's face lost its tense rigidity, and her skin seemed to turn a soft almost translucent pink.

Helen put her cup of hot coffee into the saucer. Carmie stopped balancing her knife between two fingers while it softly tapped on the table. Jamal reached for Kristen's hand under the table and pulled her closer to him. The words came into Carmie's and Helen's minds seconds before Kristen said, "I'm pregnant."

"Oh, my heavens," Helen said. She looked lovingly at her daughter's face, but Kristen did not look at her.

"Yikes," Carmie said.

"Jamal?" Helen leaned forward to make eye contact with Jamal.

He smiled broadly. "I am very happy, Helen," he said. "May I call you Helen?"

"Yes, my goodness," Helen said. "Unless it's Mom."

"We're not married," Kristen said archly.

"Okay. Okay, Kristen," Helen said a little crisply.

"Earl Gray, two spoons honey," the waitress said, putting Kristen's tea before her on her way to take orders at another table.

"We can't do this," Kristen whispered to Jamal loudly enough for everyone to hear.

"Kristen," Jamal said softly, rubbing her cheek. "It's the best way. It will be fine."

"Kristen," Helen said. "I'm very happy for you." She looked over at Jamal. "For Jamal. We'll make it all work out."

"When?" Carmie said.

"As soon as they're ready to move in," Helen said.

"No. When is the baby due?" Carmie looked at Jamal.

"Mid-July," he said.

"Oh, so soon," Helen said. She looked at her daughter. "I know you've got a big shirt on, but you don't seem that big now, what would it be, about two months from now?"

Kristen nodded her head, but did not make eye contact with her mother.

"We'd like to move in next week," she said.

"Well, I'll drive in to get you," Helen said. "How much stuff do you have?"

"No, Helen, don't worry," Jamal said, "We have hardly anything."

"You'll be okay until next week?"

"Yes," Kristen said emphatically. "I have to say good-bye to my friends," she said. "They've been my family all these years. Nine years now."

Helen's head jerked forward as if she'd been hammered on the head.

"Really eight. That first year you were back and forth."

Carmie put her arm through Helen's arm. "It's okay. It's all okay," she said.

Helen nodded.

"Whatever," Kristen said. "I left home when I was eighteen."

"Ran away," Helen said.

"Left, ran away," Kristen said. "Whatever. I'm twenty-seven now. I've been on my own for nine years. You just have to face that, Mom."

Helen nodded assent.

"Kristen," Jamal whispered to her. "Be kind, love."

"I can't do this if I can't be me," she said loudly.

"Kristen," Helen said. "You can be yourself; I promise. You can be all of your wonderful self. I'm just so happy that I'll be able to see you, and see the baby." She looked at Jamal, whom she had come to like during this meeting.

Kristen, for the first time, looked her mother in the eyes. "Okay, Mom," she said.

Chapter Twenty-Five

"Oh, Christ, Carmie. Sorry, sorry. Oh, God. Sorry again," Helen leaned on Carmie's arm as they made their way to Carmie's bus.

Kristen and Jamal were long on their way to wherever they were going, having left the diner ten minutes earlier than Carmie and Helen.

"Oh, shit, will do, Helen," Carmie said. She adjusted her stance to better support Helen's weight.

"Okay, look," Carmie said. "It's a triumph, really."

"Some triumph," Helen interrupted. "She's obviously way wacked out psychologically. She hasn't been treated in years. It's probably gone into schizophrenia or at least some other really difficult psychosis by now."

"Yeah, it looked that way. But the baby."

"Will the baby be harmed by her psychological condition?" Helen asked.

"Not a doctor, Helen. Just a soon to be former nun."

"At least Jamal seemed really wonderful."

"And balanced."

"He's clearly propping Kristen up," Helen said. "I liked him a lot. Wonder what his background is."

"To be discovered." Carmie crinkled up her nose at the thought.

"Geeze Louise, a baby in July," Helen said. "What will it be like to have a baby in the house?"

"You'll have to clear out all those bedrooms you have upstairs."

The two fell quiet until they reached Carmie's bus.

What was unspoken in Helen's mind was how will I continue with Dick?

What was unspoken in Carmie's mind was she may have to give up whoever was in her bedroom the other day.

They spoke little on the drive home, partly because Carmie had to concentrate, and partly because Helen couldn't keep up with the thoughts running through her head. She felt as if weights were on her arms and legs, and she was tired when Carmie dropped her off. She went straight to her bedroom, dropped on the bed and didn't stir all through the night.

The first thing Helen did when she woke up was walk through her house. She hadn't called Dick the night before, but before she called him this morning, she wanted to play out in her mind whether she actually had the room for a couple and a separate nursery and then enough privacy for Dick to visit. Her master bedroom was spacious. Would she have to give this to Kristen and Jamal?

They were a couple, and she was a single. Sort of.

So where would she have her bedroom?

She walked down the long hallway that led to the other bedrooms on the second floor, pausing at two large and airy bedrooms, one on either side of the hall. She opened the door to the room on the left and went in. The room had a double bed, a vanity and a Japanese silk screen that had been Hank's mother's. Helen used the screen to hide boxes filled with Mrs. Di Palma's personal things like jewelry boxes and perfume bottles Hank had been unwilling to part with. Now the screen hid boxes of Hank's personal things that Helen was unwilling to part with. Kristen and Jamal could stay in this room. It had the most space, large airy windows and yet it had privacy, and the original yellow pine floors were in good condition. She closed the door to that room. The room across the hall from this one was also used primarily for storage. This room was smaller than the one opposite it. It got the shade from the trees in the front, which would work for the baby. A changing table and dresser would easily fit and Helen might get one of those new glider chairs rather than a rocking chair for Kristen to nurse the baby in. Helen was starting to get excited about decorating this room. She closed the door to the room and looked catty-corner on the opposite side of the hall.

This room was now her office, but it had been Kristen's room and was the nicest of all the rooms on this hall. It looked out on Helen's wildflower gardens It had built in maple shelving and drawers and a window seat near the large window. Kristen had always loved this room. After she had been missing for about three years, Helen's therapist suggested accepting Kristen's unlikely return and transforming her former bedroom into an office. Helen took six months to accept transforming this room as not only useful but part of her therapy, of focusing on her life instead of Kristen's life. In the years this room had been Helen's office, she'd come to love it and find comfort in it. She'd installed Alexa here and listened to opera while she edited her manuscripts. She'd had maple bookshelves built straight across one wall, and they were loaded with her hundreds of books. It didn't seem feasible that she could change this room back into the sweet simple room it had been while Kristen grew up.

Further down the hall, there were two very small rooms opposite one another. The rooms had little light, and there was a slightly eerie feel to them that ruled them out as candidates for bedrooms for her daughter and grandchild.

She walked back to her master bedroom suite and called Dick.

She told him about parts of her meeting with Kristen, but kept some moments to herself.

"So, want company tonight?"

"Yes, I think so," she said.

Early in the evening, Helen heard the motor of Dick's Porsche as he pulled up to her house, and she went to the front hallway to wait for him, watching out one of the vertical windows alongside the front door. She saw him hop out of his car, looking excited, like a young man of twenty-five, carrying his bottle of wine, and, oh, look at that, a huge bouquet of green hydrangeas, which she'd told him last week were her favorites.

Dick's steps up her walk were like a lilt in a voice.

He's smitten with me. She smiled.

She had a big smile for him as she opened the door wide, and their kiss was much longer than a hello peck on the mouth.

After dinner, Dick asked, "So how was it with your daughter?"

Helen told him more about the years of Kristen's illness: the undiagnosed Lyme Disease that went into a still undiagnosed but observable psychological disorder, her life on the streets of Manhattan, her own chasing Kristen through those streets, Carmie's help, their recent visit at the diner, and finally, Kristen's request to move back home, pregnant and either schizophrenic or psychotic, and with her lover, Jamal.

"Oh, complications," Dick said when Helen finally stopped talking.

"Uh, huh," Helen said. Then she reached over to Dick and grabbed him in her arms. She pulled him to her.

"But it will all work. Don't think of leaving," she said. "I have come to need you."

It was now clear to Helen that she would be keeping her bedroom.

Chapter Twenty-Six

Dick couldn't see Helen for the next two days because he was taking Patsy into New York for tests her doctor ordered. It was clear to Helen that Patsy, who arranged her life to demand little from Dick, came first when she did have a need.

Helen had always come first with Hank until their own sick years when they lost every human feeling except hope for the well-being of their daughter. She was unaccustomed to having someone come before her, but she liked the space there was between Dick and her, and she so admired Patsy she wouldn't have Dick's priorities be any other way. If he had short-changed Patsy to be with her, she would lose respect for him right away and with that, he would no longer be as attractive to her.

When he got back home after Patsy's tests, he called to ask her if she'd like to go to the carnival in a nearby town.

She had missed him.

"Do they have a roller coaster?" Helen asked.

"Not sure. Doubt it. They'll have a Merry-go-round and a Ferris wheel or two."

"Bound to have cotton candy and hot dogs, right?"

"Fried pickles," Dick said.

"Banana Split Funnel Cake," Helen countered.

"Caramel apples."

"Umm," Helen said, "Oh! Kettle corn."

"Corn dogs,"

"You dog!" Helen yelled. "Wait, wait a sec. It's coming. Ahh, frozen custard. I win," Helen chortled.

"You do." Dick said. "You are a winner. So, pick you up in an hour?"

"Good deal."

In the mood for frivolity, Helen dressed in capris, a T-shirt and got an old wide-brimmed straw hat from the top of her closet. When was the last time she wore this? Then she remembered. It was to a picnic one of Kristen's classmates had in the 5th grade. Mothers were invited though that wasn't popular with the kids. Helen had bought this hat for that picnic.

It might haunt my head all day if I wear it.

Nah. Not today. I will stay just where I am, happy. I will eat all that horrible food, walk around on Dick's arm, and be his date today and not Kristen's mother for once in a lifetime. Oh, geez, I wonder if Dr. Levin's right that I can have a life.

For the past two weeks during her therapy session, Dr. Levin had said that she suspected Helen was pulling out of depression and might be entering the acceptance phase of her grieving over Kristen. Helen hadn't believed she would ever pull out of depression, but she had noticed that colors seemed brighter to her.

Maybe, just maybe.

There was a loud knock on her front door. In a few minutes, she was sitting beside Dick in his Porsche.

"How is Patsy?" was the first thing Helen said to Dick.

Dick looked over at Helen and took her hand.

"Mind if we don't talk about it?"

"Of course, I don't. I like Patsy, and I am concerned. That's all."

Dick nodded as he drove.

"Thanks," he said, squeezed her hand, and then brought her hand up to his lips. "Thanks."

There was a moment of silence in the Porsche. Then Dick started talking again.

"Breathing issues," he said between clenched teeth. He took Helen's hand again and shook it gently back and forth, a gesture that said to Helen it hurts and let's leave it here and move on to a different subject.

"So what rides are you keen on?" Helen asked.

"Ah, now you're talking," he said. "If, just if, there is a roller coaster, that's first." He looked quickly at her to see if she agreed.

"You are going alone," she said. "Haven't been on a roller coaster since high school. Hey, you should know! I went with you and when I got off, I threw up, all over…"

"Me," he finished. "You threw up all over me. Ah, yes, I remember that." They were high-spirited, giggling now.

"You led me right into that." Helen laughed.

"I did," Dick said as he wheeled the car into the bumpy dirt lane that eventually led to a parking spot, he'd been told by the parking attendant.

"Okay, race you to the teacups," Dick said, opening his door.

They both jumped out and jogged a few steps but then slowed to a saunter, hand in hand.

After walking around the grounds, the went on six rides when they stopped for a lemonade and cotton candy. They walked over to a picnic table at the edge of the carnival and were watching people scramble into lines, and kids dart from one ride to another, their parents calling after them.

Helen was glad she'd brought her hat. They weren't in full sun, but even in the partial shade, it was hot. Her sunglasses made her feel remote from the crowds, and she and Dick had temporarily run out of what seemed to both their endless conversation.

Lollygag was the word that came to Helen's mind about what she wanted to do the rest of the afternoon. It was a word her mother used when she wanted Helen to hurry and get ready for something.

"Quit your lollygagging," she'd say, which meant Helen had to go into gear. Dick, in this spot with the tree leaves bringing cover from the sun and then blowing back toward the tree, in this dappled light, made Helen feel content for the first time she could remember.

"I'll be damned," Dick said.

He'd spoiled everything by talking. "What?" Helen asked.

"Look at the merry-go-round," he said.

"I don't think my eyes can reach that far," Helen groaned.

"You don't want to miss this," he said.

Helen raised her head up from its soft slouching position and turned to look over at the merry-go-round.

She squinted but saw nothing to look at.

"What," she asked Dick.

"Wait a sec. It's just coming around again. The ostrich in the center and the zebra on the outside."

Helen watched two horses, one white and one brown, go up and down as they came around the bend. There was a giraffe and a hippo, both carrying small children. There it was, the ostrich and the zebra.

"Carmie and Sonia!" Helen called out.

As she watched them go around, Sonia on the zebra leaned over to Carmie on the ostrich going up and down. She appeared to whisper something in her ear.

"Good God," Dick said.

"What," Helen asked.

"Sonia just kissed Carmie."

"No, silly. She whispered something to her."

"She kissed her, Helen."

"No I'm sure you are wrong," Helen asserted.

"Okay, I'm wrong," Dick said.

Chapter Twenty-Seven

Moving day had come. Dick had offered to help, but Helen thought it wiser to keep the cast of characters the same as it was for the diner meeting. Her brother, Paul, had flown in early in the morning to help, but he, too, thought only Helen and Carmie should pick up Kristen and Jamal. He took directions from Helen about what furniture to move where in the house so that the rooms Helen had designated for Kristen and Jamal would be ready when they got back. He kept saying he wanted Kristen to be comfortable, and Helen kept thinking *I wonder if he'll feel that way when you get a taste of her tongue.*

Helen and Carmie left early in the morning to pick up Kristen and Jamal in front of the AMC on 84th and 6th Avenue. On the ride in, before they got to any highways where Carmie required silence, Helen said she'd seen Sonia with Carmie at the carnival the day before. She saw Carmie's head lurch forward slightly, but then she relaxed her head and sat up.

"Yeah. It was a really nice carnival, don't you think?"

"Oh, yeah. Very nice. I didn't know you knew Sonia."

"Well who gave a party a few weeks ago where we were both guests?" Carmie asked.

"Oh, Lord, that's right," Helen said. "And don't be sarcastic all day."

"Who were you with?" Carmie asked.

"Dick," Helen said.

"Tends to drop things, I think," Carmie said mischievously.

Helen looked at her and then remembered that when she'd come over the other night, Dick had been upstairs in the bedroom and dropped a book or something that alerted Carmie someone was upstairs.

"Well aren't you so smart." Helen laughed.

"Yup," Carmie said, "So what's with this brother of yours."

"I like him a lot," Helen said.

"You aren't, say, frightened of him."

"You mean because he's a murderer?"

"That's what I had in mind." Carmie smiled.

"Mitigating circumstances," Helen said earnestly.

Carmie swung her head to look at Helen. She was dead serious.

They were just getting on a highway, so both fell silent. It was a mildly sunny day, not at all like the day they'd met Kristen and Jamal at the diner. They rode in silence for about forty-five minutes and arrived near the front of the AMC.

Kristen, again in layers, looked pregnant this time, which shocked Helen, whose next thought was that she'd buy her some new maternity clothes. Then she reflected that Kristen was unlikely to wear them if only because Helen bought them.

Carmie screeched to a halt, throwing Helen forward. Carmie said, "Stay here," got up and walked quickly to the back of the bus, raised the back door, and only then looked up at Jamal, who was holding their one tattered suitcase.

"Toss in," Carmie said.

"Thanks," Jamal said.

Buckled into the back seat, Kristen had a sour face. Jamal's expression was mildly pleasant, and Carmie pulled back onto the road.

Helen felt enormously tense, fearing Kristen's volatile temper over anything she said, so she remained fairly quiet. Carmie, as always was silent and then cursing, as she bounced through the Henry Hudson Parkway toward the George Washington Bridge.

"God, Carmie nun," Kristen said. "I'm pregnant. Can you slow down or something?"

Carmie looked in the rearview mirror at Kristen.

"I don't have an Uber license," she said. "You got a free ride to your free bed and breakfast set up, right?"

"Good God," Kristen said in an exasperated tone.

Helen was grateful that Kristen didn't know and hadn't noticed that Carmie had a glass eye because she would probably have demanded to get out of the car. Kristen had a phobia about artificial body parts.

Then Helen thought how sweet Kristen had been as a little girl, how she had good manners, and thought that if Kristen had been in any way who she had been, she would still be her daughter. Helen's throat clogged, and she told her mind, NO! Stop thinking that and in a minute had control again.

"Jamal, tell me about yourself," Helen hurriedly said. "Where did you grow up?"

"East Orange, New Jersey, ma'am."

Carmie looked in her rearview mirror and saw Kristen roll her eyes at the *ma'am*. Carmie was forming a definite opinion of this girl.

"Family?" Helen said.

"Mom!" Kristen said, "have you even thought this might not be easy for Jamal to talk about?"

"Oh, well, I'm sorry, Jamal. Didn't mean to put you on the spot," Helen said.

"No, it's fine," Jamal said. He turned to Kristen, "It's fine, Kristen. I don't have a problem."

"My dad, he owned a graphics place. He did real well. But then he got cancer—colon cancer—when I was eleven. I guess they tried a few things, but he died a year later."

"I'm sorry, Jamal," Helen said.

"Yeah, was rough."

"So, then you lived with your mother, brothers and sisters?" Helen asked.

"Well, no brothers, no sisters. I was an only," Jamal said. "Yeah, me and my mom had a little house in East Orange. It was a Tudor, but the people who had it before us had painted it orange and turquoise." Jamal laughed. "Can you imagine ruining a Tudor like that?"

Both Carmie and Helen laughed and said simultaneously, "No!"

"I was getting about to paint it back, but my mom came down with breast cancer."

"Oh, my God," Helen exclaimed, turning around to face Jamal.

"Yeah, cancer in the air. Cancer everywhere," Jamal said.

"How is she now?" Helen said.

"Well, she's dead," Jamal said.

Helen didn't trust herself to say anything.

"See," Kristen said, "I told you you'd upset him."

"No, it's okay, Kristen. She's got to know something about me. I'm the father of her grandbaby," Jamal said.

"Thank you for that, Jamal," Helen said without thinking how her comment would rile Kristen up.

"Oh, thank you for that, Jamal," Kristen mocked Helen's voice.

They were now on local roads, and Carmie pulled over to the side of the road and slammed on her breaks.

"Now listen, Kristen," she said. "Your mother has hunted for you for years. She has agreed to have you and your," she looked at Jamal, "what did you say, friend, no, lover, live with her. She has agreed to give you all a home, you, Jamal, and your baby. You have to talk to her respectfully, or you'll have me to answer to. Got it?"

Kristen remained quiet and kept her sullen mouth shut.

Jamal did not look at her.

Carmie started up the bus again. They had one more stretch of back roads, and they'd be home.

When they arrived at the house, Carmie dropped them off. This surprised Helen who thought Carmie would join them for lunch, but it seemed the little family would be on their own for the afternoon.

Helen made a light lunch of tomato soup and grilled cheese sandwiches. She made Earl Gray tea for Kristen who took it and even said, "Thanks."

During lunch, Helen turned to Jamal, "When did your mother die?" she said.

"About when I was fifteen," he said. "Then I couldn't pay monthly, and a mortgage company took over the house." He laughed. "Ugly and turquoise and orange. Hey, if they'd let me stay, they would've had a free paint job." He laughed and laughed. "So that's when I took to the streets. Hey, I'd done East Orange, so I went into Manhattan. That's where I met Kristen. My lady," he said, and took her hand to kiss.

Helen relaxed.

This may work out fine.

She was now very fond of Jamal, and she could see that he was good for Kristen, who was in very bad shape, but he made things better for her.

After lunch, Helen said she'd show them to their rooms.

"What? My old room. That's all," Kristen said.

"That won't be possible, Kristen," Helen said. "It's been converted into my office, and I've added bookshelves and all. All of my professional things are there."

Kristen first looked crestfallen. "But that's my room," she said meekly.

"And if I had any hope that you'd come back, it would still be, Kristen," Helen said. She so wanted to take this girl into her arms, but she knew she had better not.

"You were gone more than eight years, dear."

"Whatever," Kristen said. "Nothing is the same. Everything changes," she said.

To Helen that sounded like a mantra she and others on the street might have said to one another.

"Come see how you, Jamal, and the baby can be close to one another."

Chapter Twenty-Eight

Kristen's re-emergence in Helen's life was a great joy to her. It was also an enormous emotional upheaval. As her feelings grew more intense about welcoming this daughter, this stranger into her heart and home, she saw that she needed more support than Carmie could give. She thought about going back into therapy, but that wasn't what she needed either. It was during a morning she snuck in a walk through her meadow and rested on a large rock near the woods that she realized what she wanted was her family. She wanted Paul. She called him to see if he could spend a few weeks with them all. After all, it was family time. He'd been with her for a few days, and in the rush of getting rooms ready for Kristen, Jamal, and the baby, she'd asked him to drag some of old Mrs. Di Palma's furniture from what was stored in the two closed off bedrooms upstairs. She left him the keys to her car so he could go into town for crib sheets and a few other things for the baby's room that they could add to in coming days.

Helen first showed Kristen and Jamal the baby's room. When she opened the door, she had no idea what she'd see, but even as Kristen and Jamal said, "Aww," so did Helen. Paul had evidently gone shopping. The crib was not only set up but it was made up with sheets and a cotton quilt with little white bunnies all over it. Paul had gotten a bunny mobile and hung it over the crib. He'd bought a changing table and a three-drawer chest of drawers, all yellow, and placed them carefully. There was a yellow and white thick rug at the foot of the crib, but the best piece in the room was a white rocker with a thick yellow pad tied to the seat and the back and a foot rest in front of it. Kristen went to the rocker, sat and gently rocked.

"This is wonderful, Mom. Just wonderful."

"It sure is," was all Helen could think to say. "Well, let's go see your room."

They were all excited to see that room, Helen particularly excited to see what Paul had done in there.

Kristen went first and opened the door.

She took a huge step backward and screamed loudly.

"What, what," both Jamal and Helen said, pushing in to see what frightened her.

It was Paul, spread out on top of their Queen bed, just waking from Kristen's scream.

"Oh, that's your Uncle Paul, Kristen. Nothing to get upset about."

"You mean my uncle, the murderer? In my bed?"

"You don't have to put it like that. He's not a murderer anymore. Right, Paul," Helen said to her brother.

He was sitting up now and trying to fully wake. "Right. Right. Not anymore."

He stood up with a big smile and said, "Hello Kristen. Jamal. Sorry I dropped off on top of your bedspread. I was up early, and was on the go. Look, I'll let you get settled and be downstairs." He looked sheepish as he scurried out the door and down the stairs.

"What in hell, Mom?"

"Look, Kristen. You don't know him. Get to know him."

"No way."

Jamal looked uncomfortable, and Kristen saw that.

"What, you think I should get buddies with my uncle the murderer?"

Helen stood by feeling mortified by Kristen's outburst.

"Look, sweetheart," Jamal said softly. "We lived with some murderers on the street. We were friends with them. I think you give this guy, your uncle, half a chance, that's what I say."

"Hadn't thought about that," Kristen said. "Like Bucky. He killed his little brother."

"Yup, and Tash. He killed his girl."

"I forgot about that," Kristen said.

Maybe because Paul reminded her of their father, Helen got a sudden image of her father listening to all this and then saying brightly, "Well, let's go forage for some good rocks."

"Well," Helen said brightly. "Do you like the room?"

"Yeah, it's nice," Kristen said. She looked all around, at the bright yellow chenille bedspread, the four toss pillows, the two sturdy backrests. She went over and passed her hand over the mahogany dresser for Kristen and Jamal's matching higher dresser that Paul had hauled across the hallway from Hank's mother's stash. The dark mahogany rocker in the room was also old Mrs. Di Palma's.

Kristen seemed about to go to the rocker when Jamal said:

"You know, Kristen, I think we should go down and really meet, maybe spend some time with your Uncle Paul."

"Oh, yeah. okay," she said.

"And when you meet your uncle," Helen said, "I'd like you to thank him for everything in these two rooms."

Kristen turned her head to the side in question.

"He flew in this morning at 8 a.m. and while we were away, he bought or found everything in both of these rooms, and put them all together better than Martha Stewart."

Chapter Twenty-Nine

The next day, Helen thought she should stay out of Kristen's and Jamal's hair and let them settle in. Anyway, from the lack of sound at the end of the hall, they were sleeping in. Paul, bedded down on the sitting room couch, was also sleeping in, Helen discovered as she made herself some coffee.

Helen had completed one of her editing projects but was only about 75% finished with the second, an assignment she hadn't wanted but Sonia had given her to make up for giving an earlier assignment to that blonde editor. If she hadn't given the new hire, Penny, the manuscript that should have come to her, Helen wouldn't be late with one of them.

With hot coffee, she settled into her upstairs office and looked at what was left in her manuscript. Not that long, so she figured it would take her about three hours to finish.

She'd just settled in to the rhythm of the prose, and re-engaged with the voice in the manuscript when the house phone in this room rang. This phone had been Kristen's first phone and she'd never had it taken out.

"Yes?"

"Oh, Helen. Hi. It's Sonia."

"Sonia?"

"I know I never call you at home, or almost never, but I have to talk to you."

"What's up, Sonia?"

"It's your manuscripts, Helen. I need them."

"Oh, I know, I know. I am so sorry. I'm working on them now, Sonia."

"But this has never happened, Helen. Not in all these years, so what's going on?"

"Well, I had a cold," Helen said, thinking as fast as she could. "And I met an old friend, believe it or not."

"An old friend, Helen?"

Helen knew she sounded like a fool.

"Okay, Sonia. It isn't any of that. Let me finish the second manuscript."

"You mean you haven't finished editing yet?"

"No. But I will in two hours. Then let's meet for coffee at 'Muffins n' Stuff,' and I'll bring everything with me and explain everything to you. Is this okay?"

"Okay, Helen, but we've got to keep to this. I'm in a world of trouble with my publishers who are waiting."

"Right. 11 a.m. at Muffins n' Stuff."

"Or I'm going to plotz with you, Helen. I swear to God."

Chapter Thirty

Driving to Muffins n' Stuff, Helen saw she was going to be a good twelve or fifteen minutes later than the time she'd told Sonia. She would lie and say she'd been absorbed in editing, but Sonia knew her very well, so she would know Helen was lying.

Damn it. There's no way I can protect my life any longer. It's all got to come out.

A baby in July with a psychologically damaged daughter almost certainly would mean that Helen would have less time than a full-time editing schedule would demand.

Helen's mind was roiling, and she had no time to settle down. She hadn't felt so unsure of the job she'd done since she first started editing. As Helen entered the diner, Sonia's hands were already waving her to a table in the adjoining room in the back. Helen was wishing the distance to the table were forty times longer so that she could at least settle some of her scattered thoughts.

"Ah, Sonia, good to see you," Helen said.

Sonia looked leery and did not get up to embrace Helen in greeting. It looked certain that Sonia wanted to get down to business right away.

"So, what's new, what's going on, Helen?" Sonia didn't even wait for Helen to sit and adjust herself, get her purse settled, pull out her napkin, and have a quick glance at the menu.

"Hold on, Sonia. Let me see what I want."

"Oh, I already ordered for us." Sonia smiled as if this were an act of generosity. "Two westerns, done, fries and rye. Marmalade on the table." She pointed to the plastic jelly holder over by the salt and pepper.

"Got it," Helen said.

Sonia cleared her throat and said, "So, like I said, Helen, what's going on?"

"Oh, God," Helen said, "it's just been a run-around non-stop,"

Sonia cocked her head in an attitude of skepticism.

"Well," Helen started. A thousand things ran through her mind, but she was just too tired to keep up with them, and anyway, all of them were lies. She simply could not do that many lies.

Helen squared her shoulders and looked directly at Sonia.

"It's my daughter, Sonia. She's come home, and she's come home pregnant and with her lover."

Sonia's eyes widened, less about Helen's news than that she was sharing it.

"She's not well, Sonia. I mean my daughter. She has been very ill for years."

"I kind of figured that," Sonia interjected.

"It's untreated Lyme disease that has gone into psychological damage."

"I'm so sorry, Helen," Sonia said sympathetically.

"Yup," Helen said. "All these years, I've been dealing with this, Sonia. She evidently was infected by a tick just after sixth grade, but we didn't know it. Finally. at the beginning of tenth grade, Hank just flew her to Mayo. They ran tests, and they found it. The *borrelia burgdorferi* bacteria had run riot in her. They put her on a drip for several weeks that killed the bacteria, but by then her psychological damage was well established, and there was no going back from it."

"When we brought her back from Mayo, she just ran away. First, she ran away locally. Then, she ran further. It took me over a year to find out that she'd run to Manhattan. This nun I know runs a support group, and I started working with her. She drives into Manhattan several times a week and tracks these kids. Some of them talk to her, and she gets information about where some of them are. Oh, what am I thinking, it's Carmie. You met Carmie at my house," Helen said, noticing a slightly wry expression on Sonia's face.

"You could have told me all this, Helen, years ago."

"You're right, but I guess I thought that if people know your business, they can try to manipulate you with that information," Helen said. It occurred to her she might be getting close to the bone with Sonia over how Penny manipulated her.

"I'll say," Sonia said.

"To finish," Helen said. "A few weeks ago, Carmie went *in* as we say and got a message from someone that Kristen wanted to meet with me. We met at a diner and Kristen brought along her lover, Jamal. I like him. The two of them asked if they could move into my house because Kristen is pregnant."

"Like you need that." Sonia said.

"Maybe, I do. It might be a way to mend things. For us to get back to being a family," Helen said softly.

"Baby in two months?" Sonia said more than asked.

Helen remained silent but nodded her head. Then she looked at Sonia, about to say how do you know that the baby is due in two months, but Sonia held a finger up as a signal she would say something. Her face had turned slightly red. Uncharacteristically, Sonia was momentarily tongue-tied.

"What, Sonia? I know you're going to tell me how you know when Kristen's baby is due."

"I am," she said.

Helen took three sips of her tea to give Sonia time to begin.

"Well," she said. "You know I met Carmie at your house."

"Yeah, I saw you guys talking most of the night."

Sonia nodded, a pleased smile at her lips.

"Well, we hit it off right away."

"I saw that." Helen smiled.

"And we've been seeing each other."

"Yeah, Dick and I saw you both on the merry-go-round at the carnival."

"Oh, yeah," Sonia said. "What'd you see?"

Helen looked quizzically at Sonia and took another sip of her tea.

"Helen, don't be dense." Sonia held her upper arms close to her side but let her forearms flop out in a gesture of impatience.

"What are you trying to say, Sonia?"

"We've become a couple, Helen."

Helen just stared at Sonia who looked almost beatific.

"We're lovers, and I've never in my life been happy like this."

Helen shook her head slightly and then burst into a big smile.

"Oh, Sonia! This is good, this is good. You've been lonely for so long. This is good. Oh, Dick," she began, but then stopped, not wanting Sonia to think she and Dick had gossiped when Dick said he thought Sonia kissed Carmie on the merry-go-round.

"Dick what?" Sonia said.

"Dick and I are lovers, too." Helen leaned back and laughed.

130

Sonia laughed hard.

"I know," she said.

Helen shot back up and leaned toward Sonia, "How do you know?"

"Because he dropped something the other night when Carm went to tell you Kristen wanted to meet."

"You mean that one-eyed nun has been telling all my business all over town?" Helen laughed.

"No, no. She just tells me things that she has to, like if she's going somewhere and she wants me to know where she is, she'll tell me where she's going and why. That's why I knew about Kristen."

"Oh, for God's sake," Helen said. "And what does Dick dropping something the other night have to do with why Carmie is going somewhere?"

"It doesn't. That one slipped out of her. She was sorry she said it and made me swear never to tell."

"But you just told."

"I know. I'm thoroughly unreliable. Good thing I'm hooked up with a holy nun who can keep me honest."

Sonia laughed almost hysterically, and Helen joined her.

"Oh, Lord, you, two are going to haunt me now for the rest of my life, aren't you?"

"Every intention of doing just that."

After a minute, their laughter subsided.

"Well, I'll tell you, Helen." Sonia reached for Helen's hand. "I'm sorry you've had the life you've had. With Kristen, Losing Hank the way you did, so I'm glad you've hooked up with Dick."

Helen reached across the table and put her hand on top of Sonia's.

"And I'm sorry you've had the life you've had," Helen said.

Both then burst out laughing again.

The waitress came up to the table, looked down at their half-eaten omelets and said, "You ladies done here?"

Chapter Thirty-One

When Helen was out with Sonia, the household slowly woke up. Jamal was first. He made coffee for everyone and sat down with Husserl's *Phenomenology* that he'd picked up at the used book store on Broadway and was dying to read. When Paul woke and saw him sitting and reading at the island in the kitchen, Paul got coffee and started to go back to the sitting room.

"Hey, Paul. Don't mean to be rude. Come on and talk with me."

"Hey, Jamal. I'm a pretty good reader myself, and I can see the signs of a man seriously into a book. What you got there? Ah, Husserl. You'll love him. A really close friend in the pen was a great reader. We spent a lot of time together."

Jamal looked at Paul.

"Reading books," Paul continued.

Just then Kristen came into the kitchen. She went directly to Jamal and kissed him. Then she saw the book on his lap.

"Oh, God, no," she said. "It's going to be a nose in the book all day, isn't it, Jamal?"

"No, no, I'll put it down."

"Well, Kristen," Paul said. "After you get coffee and breakfast, I was hoping we could take a walk." He looked at her huge belly. "I mean just around the grounds here and chat a little. What do you say?"

Kristen's back was to Jamal, so she didn't see the subtle raise of his eyebrows as he contemplated a few hours of quiet reading.

"Okay, yeah," she said. She got coffee and turned to Paul. "And I'm sorry for that screaming when I saw you yesterday. I was just surprised."

"No, no. I get it," Paul said.

"Thank you for everything you bought. Mom told us everything in both rooms was from you."

"No. A lot of it was your grandmother' stuff. Your mom showed me the night before."

As stilted as the breaking of ice between them was, by afternoon they'd spent several hours together, first walking around until Kristen's feet hurt and then in the sitting room on the couch. While Jamal was in Hank's old study reading, Kristen and Paul hadn't stopped talking. She told him about when she was younger and running away, saying she just didn't understand anything anymore, and that's why she had to leave, to run. She told him about some harrowing times on the street before she met Jamal and how happy she'd been with Jamal for over two years now. She told him how excited she was about the birth of her baby.

Then she said, "I'm going to die, you know. Probably going to die."

Paul turned his head swiftly to meet her eyes. "I know you've had damage from Lyme Disease, Kristen, but that doesn't mean dying, does it?"

"Yeah, I think so. In my case. I got a tumor. In my brain. It's something that is rare, very rare they tell me, but it has been linked to advanced Lyme Disease. That's what I have."

Paul looked at Kristen, stunned. "Does your mother know?"

"No, no, and, Uncle Paul, please don't tell her."

"I won't if you ask me not to."

"I'm asking that."

"Okay, but do you know you have a tumor or think you do?"

"I know. When they told me, I had chemo once, but I didn't know I was pregnant then, so after that I refused more chemo treatment, and I could have killed myself for having that one treatment so early in my pregnancy."

"But you have to have chemo, right?"

"I'm supposed to, but I said no because of the baby."

"No treatment?"

Kristen shook her head. "Because of the baby."

Paul had a large lump in his throat, but he didn't feel he could say anything about Kristen's decision.

"So, like I said, I'm going to die." She looked up. "But my baby's going to live."

Paul tried to go deep inside to gather strength. He would be honest with this young woman, this niece of his who was facing her compounding diseases so bravely.

"How do you think about that, Kristen?" he finally said.

"I don't think much about it, really," she said. "Just seems like I'm going to lose a lot of time in life."

"Yeah, I know what you mean."

Kristen looked at him quizzically.

"Well as you know I was in prison for murdering a man. I was there for 26 years and 3 months."

"Wow. A long time," Kristen said.

"We have something in common. We both lost or will lose a lot of time of life."

"Yeah, I never thought of it like that."

"But it's true, right, so how does that change the time we do have?"

"I don't know. How?"

"For me, it made the circle come quicker."

"The circle?"

"If you look at most lives, they come full circle. People start some place, with certain people, and then they expand, expand, expand the people in their lives, with school, more people, jobs, travel, but eventually, they circle back to the people they started with."

"Really?"

"Yeah, well, look at some people you know. Or if you read biographies, you see this over and over. It's sort of like a bird going out for a nice fly around the neighborhood. Then he decides to go further and soon he's flying all over the country, but at night, he always comes home."

Kristen just stared at Paul.

"That's why I found your mother. I figure every person is born to some certain people, and I figure that you can look and look but you probably won't find better people anywhere else. So that made me realize I wanted to be with my people. Might as well just stay with what you were born with. But my parents were gone when I got out, so I had only one person, your mother. So, see, it's because I lost all that time in prison that I started the fly back, to fly back home sooner. In the end most people fly back home. I'd learned that just reading and thinking in prison. And discussing all this with a special friend. When he died, I was ready to complete the circle as soon as I got out."

"He died?"

"AIDS."

"I'm sorry," Kristen said.

"It's okay. Miss him, but it's part of the circle of life."

"So, I should start coming full circle."

"It's what you think, Kristen. It's all just what you think."

"I want to talk to you for hours," Kristen said.

"I'm flying out later tonight, back to Ohio, but we can email, text, talk on the phone, and I'll be back here. I'll make a point of coming back soon."

Chapter Thirty-Two

When Helen got up the next day, Paul had left for the airport, and Jamal was out in the back yard riding back and forth on the John Deere.

"Wonderful young man," Helen mumbled as she stood in the kitchen watching him until Kristen barreled into the room full of complaints: the hallway near the baby's room was filthy. She wanted a professional cleaner in there. There was "no" food in the house, so she and Jamal were reduced to eating stale cereal without milk because the stamp on the cartons indicated it was a day beyond the stamp for freshness.

Helen looked at her daughter making these robust demands. She didn't look well. She was very pale and thin for a pregnant woman. There was a slight yellowish cast to her skin. She thought if Kristen had been on the highest roller coaster in the world, and had it spun out of control and thrown her from its highest peak straight into one of its metal poles, instead of being bitten by a tick, the damage could hardly be worse. Helen looked at Kristen for several seconds. Who was she? What had Helen been chasing all these years? Helen had been chasing an impossible past, an impossible reversal of the facts of Kristen's life. She was gone, had been gone for years and what was standing before Helen now was only a diseased shell of Kristen, but no longer Kristen.

"We'll take care of all of that, Kristen," Helen said.

"But you'll take your sweet time doing it," Kristen pouted.

"Kristen, I'm doing everything I can do for you the best I can."

"Well maybe that's not enough. Not enough to make it okay," Kristen shouted.

Helen decided to go on with her plans to make a meatloaf for dinner. She gathered her ingredients while Kristen stood with her hands on her hips staring at Helen. Helen glanced up at Kristen.

"Why are you looking at me that way?" Kristen asked Helen.

Helen mushed her hands in the blend of ground hamburger and pork, garlic, horseradish, diced carrots, breadcrumbs and red wine.

"What way is that, Kristen?"

"Oh, suspicious, sort of."

"Would you get me two eggs from the fridge, please. My hands are covered with this ground meat."

Kristen huffed loudly and walked to the refrigerator. She got out one egg and put it on the island hard enough to break it.

Helen looked at Kristen. Helen was hotly frustrated. From her eyebrows to her lower lip, she was squeezing and biting down, so she would say nothing, but she lost the battle and blurted, "Oh, that helps."

"Oh, that helps," Kristen repeated sarcastically.

"Kristen," Helen said, exasperated.

"What?"

Helen mushed the one egg into the ground meat, thinking she'd only use one egg this time rather than ask Kristen to get another egg from the refrigerator. She vowed to herself that she would change the tone of this conversation and was searching for something neutral to say.

She laughed softly.

"What?" Kristen barked.

"It's just you're full of surprises." Helen laughed.

"Oh, yeah," Kristen snarled. "Well I got one more big surprise for you."

"Oh?" Helen said genially.

Kristen walked up to Helen's ear and screamed, "I'll be dead in a few weeks!"

Helen lifted her hand out of the meat loaf, hauled it back, and slapped Kristen hard across the mouth. Bits of ground beef spewed onto Kristen's face and into her hair as others flew several feet and landed on mixing dishes.

"Don't you toy with death!"

Kristen gasped and put her hand to her mouth.

"God!" she screamed. Then she walked around in circles.

"Jamal!" she screamed.

"He can't hear," Helen said, feeling no remorse.

"Where is he?"

"Mowing the outer fourth acre."

Kristen stood, mouth, slightly swollen and open, and howled.

"Oh, Mom," she bayed. "Oh, Mom, Oh, Mom, Mom, Mom."

Helen just watched her, still wary, but as she watched, she felt her daughter's grief surround them both.

Helen stepped closer to Kristen, who initially held her hand up to keep her back, but then, with one more deep howl, let it drop and let her mother embrace her.

"Oh, Mom," Kristen's mouth emitted a long low doleful cry.

Chapter Thirty-Three

Kristen's mood swings were costing Helen a great deal of equanimity. The next day, Dick was free, and Helen decided to spend the morning with him. She'd leave money and the key to Hank's SUV on the kitchen island for anything Jamal and Kristen needed, but she didn't want to hang around all day to be Kristen's punching bag. She had a life, too. She wanted to see Dick, then call Carmie to tell her how happy she was for her. She wanted to drive around for a while and think. *It is true*, she thought, that when you give birth to someone, you are also born as a new being, forever part of who you've birthed, but you've still got to cling to your own life.

Helen looked to see how much cash she was carrying. She had $1000 in cash upstairs in her jewelry box, which she'd kept there since Hank took her credit cards that time he went to Mayo with Kristen.

"Oh, good," she said, seeing a fifty and three twenties in her wallet. She wouldn't need to raid her jewelry box. She slapped them all down on the kitchen island and headed out the door toward her car.

Helen drove out into the countryside, speeding, windows down, just to be blown around by the summer air. She put the radio on 60s tunes, stopped at a country drug store and got a coke. When she got in her car, she made a quick call to Dick, to meet him in a few hours at one of their favorite local restaurants. Then she kept driving further into the countryside until she almost lost her way.

Helen drove back to meet Dick. Their planned breakfast had been delayed by things Dick had to finish up, so it had become a late lunch. Helen told Dick that it wasn't yet the time for him to meet Kristen. She told him about showing Kristen and Jamal their rooms, how Paul had decorated them, about slapping Kristen, and how she'd wanted to be with him to escape Kristen's impossible moods.

When it was time to say good-bye to Dick, they spent a lot of time in the parking lot kissing before they got in their separate cars. Dick followed her nearly to her house and then made a U-turn and headed back to Patsy.

When Helen opened the front door, Jamal almost rushed her.

"Is Kristen with you?" he asked, craning his head around her to see if Kristen was just slow to get out of the car.

"No, why?"

"Well, she sure as shit ain't here," Jamal said, turning on his heel away from Helen anxiously. "Sorry, Helen. Sorry for my language."

"I don't care about language, Jamal. Just forget that. Where is Kristen?"

"I thought, I'd hoped she was with you."

"Have you been all through the house?"

"Every room."

"Did you go to the outbuildings?"

"Nope. Didn't know about them."

"Come on," Helen said, going to the key rack but not seeing the keys she wanted.

"Where?" she started.

"Oh, here," Jamal said, pulling out the key ring with the John Deere key along with the keys to the outbuildings.

"Let's go."

The two fast-walked across the field to the edge of the property where the old rotting wood shed stood. The key was catching in the lock, so Jamal asked Helen if he could try it, and he jimmied it until it opened. They took a quick look in the small empty building and headed back to the house.

When they returned to the kitchen, Helen slammed the key ring on the island and yelled, "Where in hell could she be?"

Jamal remained silent and thinking.

"Are you sure you looked in every room?" Helen asked him.

He nodded yes.

"Okay, let me look. Maybe there's a place I can think of that you didn't know about."

Helen ran upstairs and first went down the hall to Kristen and Jamal's bedroom. She looked in their closet and under the bed. Their small ratty suitcase wasn't in the room. She ran across the hall to see if they'd put it in the baby's room, but it wasn't there. Helen tried to think where else in the house Kristen might have put it. She fast-walked to her room.

"Just like Kristen to stick it in my room to get rid of it," she smiled sardonically as she yanked open her closet door. Jamal joined her in her bedroom.

"Anything?" he asked.

"No," she said, deflated by seeing lots of shoes strewn on the floor of the closet, but no suitcase.

"Wait!" She had a thought and ran to her bed, raised the bed skirt, got down on her knees, and stuck her head almost fully under the bed.

"No suitcase," she said. "Jamal, where would she go? How would she get anywhere? Was there cash on the island downstairs? I put a fifty and some twenties down there in case you guys needed something while I was gone. Were they there when you finished the mowing?"

"Nope. No bills on the island," he said.

"So that probably means she went somewhere. But how far could she get on $100?"

Suddenly Helen jerked to her knees and then her feet and rushed over to her vanity. She yanked open her jewelry box on top of the vanity.

"It's gone," she said.

Kristen had taken the $1000 in cash that Helen kept there.

"This is serious." She turned to look at Jamal. "Very serious."

For three hours they twisted in agony. They called hospitals first, then the police. Helen called Carmie, and she drove over, went into the dining room away from everyone in the kitchen and called some of her sources. Helen called Dick. Patsy was doing badly, but he said to call him in the morning and meantime he'd make local calls for any information. Carmie came back into the kitchen.

When the phone rang, each of them looked at someone else in the room as if that person would take on the bad news they sensed was coming. It was Helen who moved to the phone first.

"Yes?"

"Paul?"

"What?"

"Thank God! Thank God!"

Helen fell to her knees, and her head fell to her chest, but then she stood up quickly and turned to everyone in the room, put her hand over the receiver, and said into the room, "She's with Paul. She's fine."

When Helen hung up, she told everyone that Kristen was upset Paul left. She said she needed to see him, so she'd rifled through her mother's room, found the money and flown out to Ohio. When she landed, she called Paul to come get her. Instead, he called Helen and then drove to the airport with his suitcase. When he met Kristen, he said, "Come on, kiddo. We're going home. We're both going home."

Kristen protested, but her main desire was to be with her Uncle Paul, and she was with him. She tagged along behind him while he got tickets to New York for both of them, led her through the security check and onto the plane they had just caught in time.

Chapter Thirty-Four

Helen got up early the next morning. It was Jamal who'd picked up Kristen and Paul at the airport. Helen had stayed up to see Kristen home, but she'd been spared the trip to the airport. It seemed the day might be unpleasant. Kristen had been angry but exhausted when she got back to New York. She screamed at Helen for telling Paul to bring her back, but then fell asleep quickly. Helen was furious at Kristen, but she kept her anger at bay. Now everyone was sleeping, and the house was quiet.

It was a glorious morning in an unseasonably cool early July. The sun was strong, but there was an uncharacteristic breeze coming down from the mountains and blowing away the sun's heat. Helen's magnificent large peonies were in bloom with ants all over them, but not even a covering of ants could daunt the piercing color of the dark pink blossoms. Helen determined to take a walk in the garden after she found whoever was up.

She walked into the sitting room off of the kitchen, but no one was there. Then on a whim, she walked back toward the more formal part of the house. The living room with its antiques from Hank's mother was empty and bare, and Helen thought, *barren*. She had never liked the antiques. She'd felt obliged to accept them from Hank's side of the family because of their historical value, but she decided she'd sell them and redecorate that room sometime this next year. As she came out of the living room, she noticed the door to Hank's old study was slightly ajar, so she walked down the hall further and cracked it open further.

There was Jamal, comfortably ensconced in Hank's old leather chair, his coffee on the table next to the chair, reading his book.

"Hi," Helen said, entering with her coffee.

"Oh, hi," Jamal said. "Hope it's okay to sit in this room and borrow some of Kristen's dad's books."

"Of course, it is, Jamal. Please, be comfortable in this home, it's your home too, now," Helen said.

Jamal had a troubled look on his face.

"Everything okay, Jamal?"

"Oh, yeah, sure is," he said.

"Is Kristen sound asleep now?"

"Oh, yeah. She's done in," he said.

"I've noticed how much she sleeps," Helen said, "and she doesn't look good to me. She's kind of yellowish."

Jamal looked at Helen intently.

"Oh well, I'm just a worrywart mother, that's all. I've got to lighten up." She laughed. "Hey, when you're finished your coffee, want to come see the peonies with me?"

"Oh, yeah," Jamal said. He took a large swig from his coffee mug and put it down on Hank's desk. "Done. Let's go."

"Should we see if Kristen's up? She might want to join us," Helen said.

"Naw, she'll be sleeping for a while longer," Jamal said.

"You guys up very late last night?" Helen said.

Jamal just turned and smiled at her but said nothing. Helen opened the back door off the kitchen, and Jamal held the screen door open for her. They walked over to the peony garden and the two walked up and down to see each peony in bloom. They resembled heads of states reviewing the troops except that their facial expressions were awe-struck rather than scrutinizing.

"Did you have a garden as a kid, Jamal? Did your mother keep a garden?"

"She didn't exactly keep a garden," Jamal said, "but every time her sister gave her a rose bush, she planted it outside, so we had kind of a zig-zag rose garden patch."

"Oh, so you were close to your aunt. Why didn't she ask you to live with her when your mom died?"

"Well, I guess breast cancer ran in that family cuz she passed before my mom."

"Disease is so terrible," Helen said, "I lost several years of my life because of Kristen's illness, to say nothing of her, poor child."

The two wandered away from the peony blooms and into the meadow, talking softly.

Helen turned toward Jamal. "Has she told you about her disease, about the horror of our not knowing what it was for years and years and all the while it was destroying the very core of who Kirsten is…was?"

"Yeah," Jamal said. "She told me all about that one."

"Oh, God, Jamal, those days, well years, just about killed me."

"Yeah, what doesn't kill you makes you stronger, I guess."

Helen looked at Jamal. How handsome he looked, standing with the morning sun full on his tawny face. He had suffered so much in his young life.

She looked over at a white wild rose bush and leaned over to smell some of its blooms. Jamal's words re-played in her mind. She stood erect, not moving a hand or foot, and it felt that she was not moving an eyelash.

She opened her mouth to ask, "What do you mean, *that one*?"

"Sorry?" Jamal said.

"You said she told you all about *that* one."

Jamal said nothing. He walked ahead of Helen a step or two.

"What, Jamal?"

Jamal turned to face her.

"You know, Helen," he said, "we just don't know."

"You don't know what, Jamal?"

"Okay. Okay." Jamal stopped and looked intently down at the grass near his feet.

Helen took his arm as if to steady him.

"You heard of glioblastoma, Helen?"

"I knew it," Helen said.

"Well, doctors found a link between it and neuroborreliosis?"

Helen looked straight into Jamal's eyes.

"Yeah, I know. I've read about it," she said.

"*Borrelia burgdoferi*," she said with bitterness.

"Yes," Jamal said.

"I knew this would happen," Helen began. "Kristen's luck is monumentally foul. And she knows?"

"Yes," Jamal said. He reached out for Helen's hand, and she allowed him to take it, all the while noticing how little she felt. She searched for horror, but there was none, not even a horrible shock. She'd known when she saw how bad Kristen looked. How yellow. She focused her attention down into her stomach to feel the wrenching sorrow she had felt when she was told Kristen

145

had developed psychosis and paranoia because of Lyme Disease, but her stomach was calm. She dabbed at her eyes, feeling for at least one tear, but she stopped short of touching her face when she realized her eyes were looking straight ahead calmly.

"So, when I slapped her, she was trying to tell me," Helen said more to herself than Jamal.

Jamal just dropped his head. Kristen would have told him about that.

"Treatment?" she asked steadily. Then she shuddered.

"Oh my God, the baby," she looked at Jamal.

"We won't know," Jamal said evenly, "not for a long time."

"Won't know?"

"Won't know if there's any effects from Kristen's chemo. She had chemo before we knew she was pregnant."

Helen grimaced.

"But, Helen, doctors have high hopes he'll be okay."

"He?"

"The baby's a boy."

"A boy," Helen said, the flicker of a smile in the corner of her mouth.

"A little boy," Jamal said.

"Whew, it's a lot."

"I know," Jamal said.

"Okay, then, Jamal. Let's go sit over there." Helen pointed to two Adirondack chairs under two huge old willows.

"Tell me all about it."

As they were walking toward the chairs, thoughts rushed to Helen.

"Yes, so," she said, "what's to become of this baby, your son?"

"I'll be a good father," Jamal said. "Just it's possible he won't have a mother."

"So that's why you came here? So, his grandmother could be his mother?"

Jamal looked over at Helen with guilt in his eyes.

"Yes," he said. "It was Kristen who wanted it this way," he continued. "She didn't want her child on the streets. She wanted him to have a home. She wanted you."

"Well, you'd never know," Helen started, but Jamal interrupted her.

"Yeah, I know. I know. She just has awful manners around you. I've been telling her. But she can't help that. I mean, yeah, she could have better manners, but she can't help how she feels. She feels sick most of the time. And she's afraid that she won't be here to raise her baby. I think that's why she's so mean to you. She's angry that you might be the one raising her son, not her. She feels she let you down something awful."

Helen whipped her head back toward Jamal.

"By getting sick," he said.

"She thinks SHE let ME down," Helen yelled, but Jamal interrupted her.

"Now, she thinks she'll let her son down, too."

This time when Helen dabbed at her eyes, she found tears.

"And that's just making her even crazier than she usually is," Jamal finished.

They reached the Adirondack chairs.

Jamal plopped into one while Helen stood and looked at him.

"This is what happened, Jamal. It was ME who let KRISTEN down. I'm the one to blame for all of her suffering." Helen steadied her emotions and voice and went on. "You love Kristen, don't you? I mean, you really do love her."

Jamal looked up at Helen, squarely in her eyes.

"I do. I love her and have for just about two years now."

"I can see it, Jamal. From now on, you and I are partners. Now tell me everything that has gone on and everything we will be facing together."

Jamal told Helen that once Kristen discovered her pregnancy, she had refused all treatment. Doctors told her that pregnancy can provoke tumor growth and counselled her to consider aborting the pregnancy and entering aggressive treatment.

"But she said no," Helen interjected.

"She said no," Jamal echoed. "I ask her every day, and—"

Helen interrupted him. "And every day she says no."

Jamal looked at Helen for several seconds.

"That's why this tumor grew. They'll do surgery as soon as the baby is born. He will probably be small and born early because of the exposure to chemo, but by monitoring how fast this thing is growing, they've already warned me they fear it might be too late."

"And she won't accept any kind of treatment before he's born?"

"Won't even talk about it."

"One more thing, Helen, depending on which grows faster, the glioblastoma or the baby, Kristen could die before the baby is ready to be born."

Helen listened intently to it all. She turned to Jamal.

"And then we'd lose them both?"

Jamal looked down and nodded.

"So, we don't know anything at this time," she said.

"We don't know anything," he said.

Jamal jumped out of his chair.

"Oh, jeez. What time is it? Got to get Kristen to a doctor's appointment in the city by 2."

Helen checked her cell.

"It's 11. Can you make it?"

"I've got to check the bus schedule."

"Go on and take my car or Hank's SUV, whichever. We'll talk more about this tonight."

Jamal walked rapidly toward the house.

"Jamal," Helen called to him.

He stopped and turned toward her.

"Thank you for taking care of Kristen, and the baby," she looked at him, "and thank you for telling me the truth," and then she added, "Son."

Jamal dropped his head, but Helen could see a tiny smile flickering around his mouth.

He looked up and said, "Thanks."

Helen walked back out to her Aidirondack chair and looked around her yard.

She knows it all. She knows she'll never be a mother, may not even hold this baby, or see him. She had childhood, that's all, except for Jamal's extraordinary love. For the rest, she's been the host to *borrelia burgdorferi* and that's all.

Chapter Thirty-Five

The next day when Kristen woke, Jamal wanted to get her out of the house to prevent fights with Helen. Kristen wanted to see her friends in the City, so Jamal went down to the kitchen to find Helen and ask her if he could take Hank's SUV to go to the City for a few hours.

"Take it," she said. "Tomorrow it will be yours if you're willing to go to Motor Vehicles. I've decided to turn the title over to you."

Jamal looked at Helen. "Thank you," he said. For the first time, he walked over and kissed Helen on the cheek.

"You are going to need it, Son," Helen said, putting her hand on his cheek.

Jamal and Kristen took off for the day in Hank's SUV, and Helen had the day to herself.

Helen felt a tornado of feelings: terror for Kristen, admiration for Jamal, longing for Dick, happiness for Carmie and Sonia. This emotional weather system washing through her left her nowhere to go but to circle back through all the feelings again.

Suddenly she felt a hand on her elbow and jumped.

"Got any coffee?" Paul said, kissing her on the opposite cheek Jamal had chosen.

"Two kisses and a day of quiet," Helen mused.

Paul frowned in confusion.

"I've got coffee," Helen said.

"Good enough."

Paul thought that Helen didn't know about Kristen's glioblastoma, and Helen didn't know what Paul knew.

As they drank coffee together, they were both quiet while a streak of sun came through the window and hit them both in the face.

Helen blurted, "Kristen's got glioblastoma. She'll die soon."

Paul jumped up from his seat and came around to his sister. He put his hands on her shoulder and leaned down, putting his head next to hers.

"I've got no more tears," Helen said. Then she looked at him. "Did you know?"

"Yes."

"How?"

"Kristen told me the other day, the day you were with your boss. We had a long talk that day. She asked me not to tell you. Maybe I should have."

"Well, she asked you not to," Helen said in a quavering voice. "I wonder why she did."

"I can only imagine she wants to spare you."

"She wants to spare me!" Helen said incredulously. "Believe me, for sixteen years, she has spared me nothing." Helen laughed a strange bitter laughter.

"I'm so sorry, Helen," Paul said.

"It's not her fault," Helen perked up slightly. "God knows."

"How can I help you, Helen?" Paul stood up, came around to his side of the island and sat down.

"You can't," Helen said. "At least I don't think you can."

Paul was quiet, and he looked down at his coffee cup. "Maybe we should go for a walk. Like Dad used to take us on."

"Did he take you for walks, too?"

"Sure."

"Did he talk on and on about rocks?"

"Sure."

"Okay, let's go for a walk and look at rocks," Helen said. "I'll go change. Did you bring some strong walking shoes?"

"Sure did."

Twenty minutes later, sister and brother were back in the kitchen. Helen had on sturdy walking boots. Paul had thrown hiking boots in his suitcase at the last minute, which he had on as he looked at Helen, "Ready?"

They headed out toward the old shed Hank never tore down.

"Hank always said you need to keep the outposts of a piece of land, the thing that first marked it, or you'd lose the soul of the land," Helen said.

They walked on, and Paul said, "Sort of like us keeping the first memorable activity in both of our lives, those endless walks with dad."

"What did you think of those walks, Paul?"

"At the time, I thought they were boring. I thought dad was a little bonkers, loving rocks as he did. But in years since I asked myself why I remember those walks more than anything in my early childhood. Then it came to me those walks were my anchor and dad a funny sort of spiritual guide."

"Oh, yes," Helen murmured. "So, why rocks, do you think?"

"Because they don't change. All their changing is already done, and they are what they are for the long-haul."

"At a certain point," Helen said, "people stop changing, and they are what they are for the long haul. It's just that you don't always like where they stop changing."

"Until you understand it."

"What do you mean?"

"Well, take me. I changed enormously in prison, just from being alone, from thinking, from reading, and thinking some more, and then I met Carlos and I stopped changing. I kept changing until I got some sense into my head and let love in, but once I did, I stopped changing. Thank God, I did, or who knows, I might have changed back into the fool that I'd been."

"Carlos?"

"My lover."

"Ah. Where is he?"

"Dead."

"Oh, Paul. I'm sorry." Helen took Paul's hand in her.

"It's okay. We had love, so it's okay."

"You stopped changing when you found him?"

"I think people do," Paul said. "I think people keep changing unless they find someone who embraces them wholly, just the way they are, and then they stop changing."

"I haven't stopped changing," Helen said.

"Kristen," they both said at the same time.

"Go on," Paul said.

"Has Kristen stopped changing because she has Jamal, or will she stop changing when she has her baby, if she makes it that long." Helen burst into tears, and Paul reached over and held her.

"Kristen's like two beings now. There's who she is, so lost inside her, and she is a disease, several diseases, really. I know you know this, Helen."

"Yes, I know that," Helen said, muffling tears.

"She will make it," Paul said. "She's so close."

"And then she will be stone. Stone cold dead," Helen said.

"No. Not dead, and not cold. Just stone," Paul said, thinking these thoughts for the first time. "She will just have stopped changing. She will be something solid. A touchstone for her son," Paul said.

"What do you mean?"

"Well isn't a stone a point in time when something stopped changing? When all that is in it becomes inert, solid, complete, defined, like a painting that's finished?"

Paul leaned down and picked up a gray stone that had fallen into a marshy part of the meadow. It was glistening with water on its surface.

"So, look," he said to Helen. "This water, this flowing, changing, nourishing water cannot permeate the surface of the stone. There are two worlds here: the finished and the unfinished, the solid and the flowing, really, when you look at all this, our earth, everything living lives between these two things, rock and water."

Paul walked over to a maple tree about ten feet away and then back to Helen. "So that tree is able to stand because its soil is in rock. Got to have a rock bed to anchor you. And that tree is nourished by the water that comes from the sky, as well as nutrients in the soil. One is staid, steady, firm, consistent, and gives security. The other, fluid, unpredictable, dynamic, and necessary for growth. Everybody needs something solid, a touchstone, through life, and if a parent has died, that's it. And everyone needs things that flow with them, like water. Kristen will be her child's touchstone, and Jamal will be his water. Both will be the essence of that child, and he'll be okay, Helen. He will."

"My goodness, Paul. You learned to think like this in prison? You've come out more reflective and more stimulated by what you see than any college graduate I've met in years."

"Product of Carlos's love, which freed me from being trapped by the 15 square feet allotted me to be a human being in."

"I want to find a stone for the baby. It will be for Kristen and for understanding how important stones are, as dad showed us," Helen said, wandering off near the maple tree Paul had studied. After a half hour, she leaned down and closed her hand over something she brought back for Paul to see. He opened her hand to show a pure white, perfectly round rock. "Here it is," she said, holding the rock up to the sun.

Chapter Thirty-Six

Kristen and Jamal named their son Emmanuel Jamal Henry when he was delivered by emergency C section and lifted from his mother's scrawny, yellow, sick body at 9 p.m. on July 14. He was born at thirty-nine weeks and had a robust cry though neither his nor his mother's survival seemed likely early in the night when doctors first worked on bringing Kristen back from the edge of a coma, and then Emmanuel to the brink of life.

Kristen held him and looked into his face for almost five full minutes soon after he was born. She whispered many things to him, her mother's pledge and love given with soft deep passion.

Jamal stood back, eager to hold his son, but not wanting to take even a second away from Kristen. He told her the doctors said Emmanuel looked healthy, was a good birth weight at 6 lbs. 2 oz., that he'd scored well on the Apgar, and they had every reason to be optimistic that he would grow normally.

Kristen looked intently into Jamal's eyes and smiled weakly. Then she repeated softly, "God is with us, God is with us," the meaning of Emmanuel.

Once Kristen fell asleep, Jamal left to get some food at a nearby restaurant, and Helen stepped into the hallway to call Dick about the news that Kristen and Emmanuel were both holding their own. Dick was relieved for them all and wanted to linger on the phone as much as Helen wanted to be in the room with Kristen.

Getting off the phone, Helen popped her head into Kristen's room, saw she was still asleep and walked down to the nursery, and asked if she could hold Emmanuel. The nurses told her they were scheduled to bring him to Kristen's room in about a half hour and if she were there and Kristen, asleep, that would be her chance to hold him.

Helen tiptoed into Kristen's room and sat in a chair at the foot of her bed.

Soon the nurses brought Emmanuel and placed him into his grandmother's eager arms.

Helen cooed at him and watched his eyes roam to find the origin of the sounds. His little lips opened and closed.

"Oh, you're hungry, little Emmanuel, aren't you?"

Just then a nurse brought in a warmed bottle.

"Give him all of it. He needs it now, and if Kristen wakes, we'll put him on her breast. It would be really good if he could get some of her breast milk for the antibodies."

"But is she," Helen started.

"Oh, yes. She's lactating. Not a whole lot, but enough," the nurse said. "And in case you're worried, doctor said there is no transmission of anything to do with her disease to the baby."

Helen turned back to Emmanuel.

"You have the most beautiful green eyes. Just like your mom," she said.

Then she gave him the bottle, and he sucked vigorously on the nipple.

Helen maintained a one-sided dialogue with him, pretending he was answering her.

"Oh, yes, when you are three years old, I'm going to make you a beautiful chocolate cake. Yes, I am."

Emmanuel's eyes widened as if he knew what she was promising.

"And for your birthday every year," Helen went on, "you will choose your favorite cartoon character, and I will make a cake just like that character, only for you and nobody else."

"Lucy…Snoopy," came softly from the corner of the room.

"Kristen! You're awake!"

"Yes, Mom."

"Well then, Lil Mama," Helen walked Emmanuel over to Kristen. "You're supposed to nurse him."

Helen pulled the rubber nipple from Emmanuel's mouth, and his little face screwed up in anger, getting ready for a yowl. Helen put him down on Kristen, who had pulled her gown off her breast. Emmanuel rooted at Kristen's breast and found her nipple, latched on, and sucked loudly until Kristen's milk let down. Kristen smiled when she heard his soft grunts of pleasure.

"That's your son," Helen said.

"This is my son," Kristen echoed.

Chapter Thirty-Seven

Helen and Jamal brought Emmanuel home three days later. Doctors said he was a strong baby, that he'd shown good development and was very alert. Kristen had pumped milk which Helen and Jamal gave him in a bottle. A week after Emmanuel was born, Kristen, still in the hospital, had become too weak to pump her milk, so Jamal and Helen began feeding him formula.

Helen already had plans to re-design the whole back of the house, including her office, for Kristen, Jamal and Emmanuel. She thought if she hurried and designed the suite including Kristen, then Kristen would have to live to fill it. She knew who she'd hire as contractor and was sketching plans late at night. She'd fit Emmanuel out like a king when things settled down.

After her walk with Paul, and finding the smooth round white stone for Emmanuel, she began a rock ritual with Emmanuel every night. She had first examined the white rock she'd chosen carefully, to make sure it was not so big that it could hurt Emmanuel if his foot kicked out and hit it, so Helen put it in a corner at the very end of his crib and he was too young to move himself closer to it. She also made sure it was not too small so that if he squirmed down to it, it could not fit in his mouth. She scrubbed it, poured alcohol over it, let it dry thoroughly and only then did she put it into his crib. She placed her hands over the rock and said, "I invoke my father, and I invoke your mother, Emmanuel, to give you the solidity of this rock and the fluidity of those who will live alongside you, the holy water in your life, so that you will be as strong as this earth your whole life long."

Helen was so absorbed in tending to Emmanuel that it scarcely registered that Dick hadn't called since Helen told him about Emmanuel's birth from a hospital phone. She was tired, too tired to work out in her mind what this meant, but she hoped it didn't mean that Patsy was getting worse. She missed Dick, she worried about him and his feelings for her, and there was an ache in

156

her, but it was dull and remote compared with the emotions she was harboring for Kristen and Emmanuel.

She or Jamal spent the day in the hospital with Kristen, and the other, at home with the baby. By now Kristen was sleeping most of the time. The hospital staff was arranging to transfer her to a hospice center within the week.

Helen kept trying to think when she had lost Kristen. The moment of the bite? The months and years of her pig-headed refusal to have Kristen see Hank's doctor? At her diagnosis and the news that it was too late to stop related psychosis? When she ran away? When she ran away again after they fought over mayonnaise? When? When was it? She knew Kristen was only days from death. This would be Helen's final loss of Kristen. She had been losing her in increments for sixteen years and been grieving for all those years, and would continue to grieve every day she lived, but over the years the loss had settled into her life, had become a fact, as someone who loses a leg has to accept that loss in order to learn how to walk again. Helen would always live as if she were skating on an iced-over pond. She would never know, as she hadn't for the last sixteen years, when she'd fall through the ice, or whether she'd be able to climb out of the freezing pond one more time.

In the evening, when both Helen and Jamal were home, each rushed for the phone whenever it rang, but it mostly rang for ordinary business: someone wanted to sell Helen extra insurance; someone else wanted Helen to take surveys.

The third night they had the baby home with them, Helen was tense. She'd just gotten a notice in the mail that she had to appear in Court the following week to plead on charges of assaulting her daughter in the vicinity of 84th and Broadway, and she didn't know how she would squeeze that in. She told Jamal she would go to bed early.

She fell into a deep sleep by 8:30 p.m., and her next awareness was a dream in which she was speeding in a car that went so fast she could no longer see the trees in front of her. She saw a blur of green, and she looked away from the blur just before the car banged against a wall that materialized next to it. Helen felt her head rock from side to side and woke with Jamal leaning over her, gently rocking her head up off the pillow, from side to side and back down on the pillow to wake her.

"Oh, God," Helen said groggily. "Time is it?"

"It's 3 in the morning, Helen," Jamal said softly.

"Oh, back to sleep!" she moaned and rolled over.

"Helen, the hospital just called."

Helen's eyes shot open. They stung. God, how they stung.

"What'd they want," she said in a flat voice.

Jamal just looked at her. "Helen," he said.

Helen sat upright and blinked her eyes.

"Kristen?"

"Yes," Jamal said. "About ten minutes ago."

Helen looked at Jamal intently.

"No struggle," he said. "Just calmly."

Helen slumped.

Jamal reached to embrace her, which she allowed for a few minutes.

"Okay," she said. She looked at Jamal.

He looked at her and frowned slightly. He didn't think she'd understood.

"Helen," he said in even tones. "Kristen is gone."

Helen swiveled her legs over the edge of the bed, and Jamal took several steps back to give her room.

She stood up and reached for her robe at the end of the bed and put it on.

"I know." She turned around and looked Jamal in the eyes.

"This is harder for you than me," she said. "I'm used to losing Kristen. You aren't."

She headed for her bedroom door.

Jamal said nothing, but he dropped his head on his chest.

"I hear the baby, Jamal," Helen said. "I'll go feed him."

After Emmanuel had gurgled down his bottle, fallen asleep at the last sips, and Helen had put him back in his crib and tucked him into his blanket, she could feel a well of tears surging up. *Is this the thin ice I fall through?* she wondered.

She walked down the long hall and down the stairs. She walked briskly through her kitchen and took the first two of the three steps to the sitting room at once. She picked up Dumpster who'd been sleeping in the rocking chair and sat down in the rocking chair with Dumpster on her lap. She began rocking slowly and held Dumpster as tightly as he would allow, so she wouldn't fall through the ice.

Dumpy blinked his eyes and oddly did not get up to find himself another spot. Helen wept, soft little rhythmic weeps near Dumpster's head, which he allowed.

Then she rocked harder. Dumpster jumped off her lap, and Helen called out, "Paul. Paul."

"Yeah," Paul woke from his sleep on the couch. He sat up. "Helen? What's wrong."

Helen rocked hard but said nothing.

Paul got up and went to Helen. He reached for her and brought her to a stand so that he could hold her.

"Helen," he said. "Has the time come?"

"The time has passed," she said.

"Oh, my sister," he said, and held her firmly as she wept in small gasps for a long time.

Chapter Thirty-Eight

This was the second time in two years that Helen entered the church of St. Mary of the Mount. She was in their community center often for Carmie's support groups, but never the church. Hank's funeral had been here, and though Helen didn't know the clergy well, she worked with them to make all the arrangements for his service. Carmie somehow knew Helen couldn't do that again so soon, so she made all the arrangements for this memorial mass for Kristen.

Helen climbed the first bank of four stairs to the church. Jamal had her left arm, and Paul had her right arm. She'd been nervous about leaving Emmanuel at home with a sitter Carmie had found from the congregation. Helen had insisted on hiring two sitters, one to watch the other. Jamal had wanted to stay home with Emmanuel, telling Helen that Kristen would have preferred he do that than go to some meaningless funeral of hers. Helen knew he was right about Kristen's preference, but she insisted he attend the funeral with her.

They had decided that Jamal and Emmanuel would be living with Helen for the time being and most likely until Jamal had a solid foothold in a life that would support all of Emmanuel's needs.

Helen hadn't told Jamal yet, but she intended to send him to pilot's flight school since he'd always wanted to be a pilot, and she had the means to support that dream. She would need to scale back her editing radically in the next few years to take care of Emmanuel while his father made longer-term plans for them, but Hank had left her well off.

She pushed up the black veil that hung from the ridiculous black hat she'd bought to go with her other black mourning clothes as she ascended the second bank of stairs—seven in all—that led to the great carved mahogany doors of St. Mary on the Mount. She felt like a hypocrite entering this church she never entered at other times except to go to its community center for Carmie's support groups. She'd told Carmie she wanted to speak briefly at this service though it was highly unusual for the mother of the deceased to do so. She expected some of Kristen's friends, and she wanted to warn them to be careful about *borrelia burgdorferi*.

She reached for the long heavy bronze handle to the door of St. Mary of the Mount, thinking about the flowers Dick and Patsy had sent to the church yesterday. Carmie had told her it was the largest funeral arrangement she'd ever seen. Mixed flowers, mostly yellows and white.

Paul reached to grab the handle for Helen and opened the huge heavy door. It was cool and dark inside. Helen blinked for a few seconds to acclimate herself to only candlelight.

There seemed to be hundreds of candles lit all along the pews and over to one side up near the altar. Carmie must have arranged for them. Helen looked down the long nave of the church and saw Kristen's coffin in the transept near the altar with a single large candle in a floor-standing brass holder. She had thought this sight would bring tears, but it didn't. She was steady, even tranquil as she let Jamal and Paul slowly lead her down the nave as her eyes continued to adjust to the lighting.

She looked up when they approached the first seated people, about a third of the way down the nave. Though people were scattered in various pews, far more people had come than she expected. She looked to the right.

"So sorry, Helen." It was Janet, the woman she'd had to coffee after her daughter ran away. She'd been a horrid bore at Helen's dinner party. She was reaching her hands over to Helen. Helen paused and squeezed her hand. "Thank you for coming."

In the pew ahead of them, she saw Sonia. Hearing her speak, Sonia turned around and stepped toward the aisle.

"Helen, dear friend. I am so sorry," she said.

Helen walked into Sonia's pew a step, and the two women embraced.

Then Helen joined Paul and Jamal again, and they proceeded further down the nave. She looked to the left.

A few rows closer to the altar, Helen saw the mothers of several of Kristen's old classmates, going back to the sixth grade. Jen and Sheila were sitting next to them. Sheila's second baby was a girl, it looked like, from the pink blanket she was wrapped in. She'd had good luck after all. The sight of Sheila holding her baby made Helen's throat catch, and she tightened her grip on Paul's arm so fiercely that he looked over to her and whispered, "Are you okay?"

She was about to say, "Yes," when she saw Dick and Patsy in the third row back. Patsy was all in black, and she seemed to tremble. Dick took her arm to steady her.

My God, Helen thought, *there is a brave woman.* Helen slipped her arms away from Paul and Jamal and whispered to them, "Be just a minute."

They stood still, waiting for her.

She excused herself to the one lady at the aisle, indicating she wished to slide by her to greet the couple next to her. She first greeted Patsy, taking her by her shoulders and giving her a long hug. "Patsy, you are so brave to be here for me. I want you to know how deeply I admire you."

Patsy's eyes glistened. "Oh, Helen," she said haltingly. "We can't measure our losses, can we? We just have to accept them." Patsy reached up and kissed Helen on the cheek. "You have my blessing," she whispered in Helen's ear.

Though Helen understood her, she looked down and next greeted Dick. "Thank you for coming," she said. Then she slid back to the aisle. The lady at the aisle bent backward to let her pass, and Helen once more linked her arms in the arms of Jamal and Paul. Ahead she saw the officiating priest. She had only met him a few times. It was Carmie who had asked him to officiate at the Mass. He was young looking though Helen suspected he was older than he looked. She had heard he was a good man. She knew he had guided Carmie in renouncing her vows. Father Hugh Finnegan was his name.

Then she saw Carmie, dear wonderful Carmie, who had been so stalwart through Helen's hell. Helen raised a hand slightly to blow Carmie a quick kiss, but Carmie ducked her head.

Such a toughie. Helen smiled before she sat down in the first row between Paul and Jamal.

Father Finnegan began at once, "Receive the Lord's blessing. The Lord bless you and watch over you. The Lord make his face shine upon you, and be gracious to you."

Suddenly there was a loud clamber at the back of the church as a large number of young adults, some in cut-off jeans and others with cells beeping and ringing, entered the church, still talking and laughing to one another as they bumbled forward, looking for seats.

"Yo, Monsignor," an unruly looking boy called out, "sorry to be late but the L14 was twenty-five damned minutes late."

The congregation murmured, and laughter sprouted from different directions.

Once all of the kids, the kids Kristen had lived among for eight years, had found seats and waved to Jamal up front, Father Finnegan gently laughed and said:

"Welcome! You are children of God, and may the Lord look kindly on you and give you peace; In the Name of the Father, and of the Son and of the Holy Spirit."

When the Mass had ended, but before Father Finnegan said, "Let us go in peace to live out the Word of God," he said, "Kristen's mother, Ms. Helen Baird, would like to say a few words, and I invite her into the pulpit so that she may be heard."

Helen gathered her notes and slowly mounted the steps of the pulpit. She hadn't known until Carmie told her the day before that lay people are not allowed in the pulpit, and she liked this priest for dispensing with whatever rule he dispensed with. She liked everything about his service, especially the way he welcomed Kristen and Jamal's street friends but also his sermon, and the words he'd said about the sanctity of Kristen's life. She'd been moved by it all, so found herself more emotional than she'd felt in months, which shattered her confidence.

She reached the top of the pulpit and just looked around.

So many people who must have cared about Kristen.

"Maybe I made a mistake saying I wanted to speak," she laughed gently, and the crowd in the church laughed with her.

"But I do want to tell you a few things, from me and on behalf of Kristen's devoted father, Henry Di Palma," she continued, her voice under control.

"Please do not feel sorrow for me, for us," she said. "I lost Kristen years and years ago, and so it is an old loss, a dull ever-lasting ache, but no longer sharp and cutting. I lost her, as most of you know, to *borrelia burgdorferi*, the bacteria that ticks carry and that cause Lyme's disease, and if that Lyme's disease goes untreated, as Kristen's did, for years and years and through ignorance about it, it can cause severe psychological disorders, which Kristen suffered from. So I ask all of her friends," and Helen looked to the rear of the church where Kristen's street friends were sitting, "please, if you go into

163

woods, or even into one of Manhattan's parks, check yourselves right away, and if you see a round spot like a bull's eye anywhere on your body, go to a clinic and have a doctor look at it. Do this," she said, "for Kristen."

Helen heard intermittent sobbing, but she tried to ignore it so she could finish her comments without breaking down herself.

"Also," she said at a measured pace, "I want you to know that at the end of her days," Helen choked but then quickly cleared her throat while the sobbing she'd heard became louder, "Kristen had great joy. She had the love of an extraordinary man." Helen paused and looked out over the pews. "Many of you know Jamal." From the far back of the church, she heard someone yell, "Hey, Jamal baby! You fly!" and calls of "Yesssss," and "Amen." From older parishioners, applause, which subsided as soon as she raised her head to look out over the pews again.

She coughed, cleared her voice and continued, "I have gotten to know, and," she looked directly at Jamal, "love him in these recent months." The kids at the back of the church applauded. Adults joined them. It wasn't clear whether this applause was for Jamal himself or for Helen's new-found love for him. "And," Helen said firmly to tone the applause down so she could continue, "I've received a great gift of having my brother, Paul, join my life after many years of absence." The applause started all over again. Helen turned and addressed Paul, "I love you, Paul." Paul's head dropped swiftly as if to hide tears that may have been in his eyes.

Helen shifted her weight from one leg to the other. "Kristen, Jamal, Paul, and I welcomed Emmanuel Jamal Henry just a few weeks ago, and he is the most," Helen paused for her word, "delicious creature on this earth." The entire congregation laughed in fits and starts.

Helen was feeling herself well up, but she couldn't stop now. "I want you to know," she gained equilibrium, "that Kristen was able to hold him, to nurse him, to fall in love with him, and that was her last experience on earth." Now Helen was fighting hard to keep tears back, but she went on with a practical thought, *and Jamal and I are going to co-parent him,* she laughed softly, *until Jamal gets sick of me.* There was again laughter from the congregation. "But until then," she smiled, "I will have the miraculous experience of becoming a mother again as a grandmother." There was soft murmuring among the congregation.

"So," she said, looking to the rear of the church, "never count out older folks," she laughed, "because you may need them one day." A round of laughter went through the congregation and just as it seemed to end, someone said something Helen couldn't hear, and the laughter started again. She paused and looked over the congregation while the laughter dwindled.

"Thank you," she said, "for coming today for Kristen, for Jamal, for Emmanuel, for Paul, her uncle, and for Hank and me, her parents."

She looked down on Kristen's casket and hurriedly climbed down the pulpit stairs before erupting in tears.

From the center of the Sanctuary, Father Finnegan shouted, "Let us go in peace to live out the Word of God, oh yes, and God bless those who came from the City even though the bus was twenty-five damned minutes late."

Chapter Thirty-Nine

Three months later, Sonia and Carmie had a party to celebrate their Domestic Partnership Registration, which they'd filed the week before at the City Clerk's office on Worth Street. They'd stopped short of marriage because Carmie thought marriage was a wussy straight trap, always humiliating for women. But they'd had to do something after Carmie renounced her vows and left the convent because then she had no health insurance. A Domestic Partnership allowed her to be on Sonia's health plan.

Both Carmie and Sonia thought they were being reckless for becoming a couple when they did. After meeting at Helen's dinner party, where they'd found tons to talk about, they'd begun a tight friendship, which is where both intended to keep it.

Sonia had known for years she was attracted to women, but she never had confidence to do more than flirt with the likes of Penny.

Carmie had spent her life in an asexual manner once she came in off the streets of Manhattan where she'd been promiscuous. When she lost her eye to a beating one of her male lovers gave her, she turned against her sexuality, considering it destructive and dangerous, and determined to live a celibate life in the sisterhood.

It was the day Carmie and Sonia went together to the county carnival that the sensual undertones of their friendship took on a life of their own. and their lively friendship erupted into romance.

They were riding the merry-go-round, Carmie going up and down on an ostrich when suddenly, Sonia, on a zebra, was stirred to try holding the ostrich back from rising again in order to kiss Carmie on her lips. This was the kiss that Dick had seen.

From that point, Sonia and Carmie decided there was no reason to hold back, that both had been denied, or she had denied herself pleasure, happiness through much of life. Seeing there was less of life than more for them to live, they wanted to live it fully. They were too old for caution and should love without restraint. *And why*, they thought, *shouldn't they?* Each had had a childhood of terrific suffering, which had set up lives lived in despair. They were done with denying themselves. That is why they were having a party in the same park where they fell in love, and though the carnival had left town, they both carried images of the merry-go-round in their eyes, so they rented a bright yellow and white tent for this party, hired a caterer with a décor expert on staff, who'd filled the tent with balloons and ordered a huge layered cake with yellow icing and a bright red, yellow, green and blue merry-go-round on top.

Sonia wore a gold metallic bandage dress, plus size. Helen hoped she felt sexy as she smiled at Sonia's protruding belly. Her hair was once again haystack blonde, but her carefree, exuberant gestures that day brought color and with it, beauty into her face.

Carmie wore a Logan green pants suit with a white shirt under it. No glitter for her. Helen thought she looked more like a nun this day than when she really was a nun, running around in jeans and sandals when off duty.

There were trays of hor d'oeuvres passed around by two hired college students: fancy crudities, cheese and charcuterie, fig bites, caviar on grape leaves, black garlic creamy cheese and more. There was a wheel of shrimp, crab legs, and lobster tails which spun around over a platter of ice. Slices of filet mignon, Smithfield ham, and Stuffed Chicken Valentino, served at the head table. There was a salad bar and next to it, a vegetable bar that had green beans, broccoli, and asparagus prepared in sauces. There was a bar serving The Macallan Scotch, The Botanist Islay Dry Gin, Maker's Mark Bourbon, and Jean-Marc XO Vodka. Glasses of Taittinger champagne were circulating on a tray.

Though their culinary offerings were extravagant, their friendships were meager. Sonia, who was paying for all this, would not go bankrupt because there were only about thirty people there. Spencer Samuelson and his wife, Babette, came. Dick and Helen were there. Sonia claimed Helen for her "side," because Carmie had a few more guests than she did. Father Hugh Finnegan came as did Sister Rosalie, who when the chips were down for Carmie, had helped her make a dignified exit from the convent. Carmie had heard there was a brief incident of fisticuffs between Sister Rosalie and Sister Maureen, and truth or rumor, from the day Carmie heard that, she loved Sister Rosalie. Fred Unger was there, but Helen couldn't figure out why except that he seemed constantly in need of a meal. Jamal "wore" Emmanuel, now four and a half months, in a baby sling that let Emmanuel give everyone a broad drooling smile, and Carmie's mother, now in a wheelchair, had been pushed into the tent by Father Finnegan, and placed near the serving table. Paul had accompanied Dick and Helen.

Helen walked up to Carmie and gave Carmie a kiss on her forehead before Carmie could stop her, and rejoined Dick.

Pretty soon, voices were bouncing off tent walls as guests tried out several of Sonia's excellent choices in liquor and champagne. When Sonia greeted Father Finnegan, she spoke so loudly that all the guests heard her say, "My poor Jewish Mum would have croaked if I'd ended up with a former priest, that's for sure."

Father Finnegan responded, "But a former nun is okay?"

"Hell, no, but Mum's already croaked."

When the group was fairly tipsy, people gave toasts. It turned out that Spencer wasn't half bad. He toasted Carmie and Sonia: "You two give marriage a bad name, only because you didn't choose it. I am so happy to see Sonia happy after years of doing nothing but work. A creasy smile played over his mouth. Of course, Sonia, if your work output falls, you're fired!"

Everyone laughed hard. Then Spencer became sentimental. "Sonia, we love you, and may you plaster that smile across your face always."

"Yeah, she's pretty plastered," Carmie chimed in.

Carmie's mother raised her glass. "To my daughter. I'm glad you are happy," she said from her wheelchair in a frail voice that most couldn't hear.

Murmurs of "What?" "What'd she say?" went around the tent for a few seconds.

Father Finnegan then held his glass up. "Hear, here, Mrs. Coviglio. I am, Sister Rosalie is, we are also very happy that Carmie has found the person who will be her companion through the rest of life. God bless you, Carmie. May you immerse your life in love."

Helen knew at some point she would be expected to propose a toast, something like wishing great blessings and hopes for the new couple, even love.

That time was now.

She reached into the pocket of her dress and held something in her left hand. In her right hand, she held her glass out in front of her.

Although Kristen's death still stole her most positive emotions, Emmanuel had mercifully been born. Dick told her he loved her, and she loved him. She and Paul had found one another. All is well, love conquers, yet remaining was an insidious forewarning: there is something terrible about love.

Dauntless, a tiny smile managed to brush across Helen's face and vanish like a whisper, yes, even Bambi will live another day.

Helen squeezed her left palm where a smooth white rock lay hidden.

In her right hand, Helen raised her glass high.

CPSIA information can be obtained
at www.ICGtesting.com
Printed in the USA
BVHW052058261222
654966BV00011B/383